Also by Larry Niven

Destiny's Road
Ringworld's Children
Rainbow Mars
The Draco Tavern
N-Space
Playgrounds of the Mind
Scatterbrain
Stars and Gods

With Edward M. Lerner

Fleet of Worlds
Juggler of Worlds
Destroyer of Worlds
Betrayer of Worlds
Fate of Worlds

With Steven Barnes

The Descent of Anansi
Achilles' Choice
Saturn's Race
Dream Park
The Barsoom Project
The California Voodoo
Game
The Moon Maze Game

With Jerry Pournelle

Inferno
Escape from Hell

With Jerry Pournelle and Steven Barnes

The Legacy of Heorot
Beowulf's Children

With Brenda Cooper

Building Harlequin's Moon

With Gregory Benford

Bowl of Heaven
Shipstar*

*forthcoming

THE GOLIATH STONE

**Larry Niven and
Matthew Joseph Harrington**

A TOM DOHERTY ASSOCIATES BOOK
NEW YORK

This is a work of fiction. All of the characters, organizations, and events portrayed in this novel are either products of the authors' imaginations or are used fictitiously.

THE GOLIATH STONE

Copyright © 2013 by Larry Niven and Matthew Joseph Harrington

All rights reserved.

A Tor Book
Published by Tom Doherty Associates, LLC
175 Fifth Avenue
New York, NY 10010

www.tor-forge.com

Tor® is a registered trademark of Tom Doherty Associates, LLC.

ISBN 978-0-7653-6889-8

Tor books may be purchased for educational, business, or promotional use. For information on bulk purchases, please contact Macmillan Corporate and Premium Sales Department at 1-800-221-7945, extension 5442, or write specialmarkets@macmillan.com.

First Edition: June 2013
First Mass Market Edition: June 2014

Printed in the United States of America

0 9 8 7 6 5 4 3 2

Prudence is the belief that bad things have preventable causes.

Paranoia is the belief that it's all the same cause.

Politics is the belief that you know what the cause is.

I would sooner believe two Harvard professors
would lie than that stones may fall from Heaven.

—*FALSELY ATTRIBUTED TO THOMAS JEFFERSON*

Ignorance is preferable to error; and he is less
remote from the truth who believes nothing, than
he who believes what is wrong.

—*THOMAS JEFFERSON*

Look! Up in the sky!

—*JERRY SIEGEL*

Cast and Crew

Bigfeet:

JUAN HENCKE—*Director of a university astronomy department*

TED MENDEZ—*Actual astronomer*

TOBY GLYER—*Engineer, physician, and creator of life, but easy to get along with*

ABDALLAH CHAHINE—*Very ill traveler of Egyptian birth. Also chief auditor, Aswan Dredge Project. Poor digestion.*

MAY WYNDHAM—*Rocket scientist, test pilot, idealist*

GORDON WYNDHAM—*Financier, engineer, idealist*

BERT CRASSEN—*U.S. senator from Michigan, falled writer, chairman of Internet Regulatory Committee. Soylent.*

JANE BODINE—*U.S. representative from Arkansas, recycling heiress, three times widowed. Soylent.*

FRANCES HILL—*Agent provocateuse. Former prostitute.*

RORY DENNETT—*News performer, CNN*

WADE CURTIS—*Author, engineer, historian, commentator, veteran, genius*

CHARLES OPIE—*Marshall, United States Department of Homeland Security (U.S. DHS)*

WILLIAM CONNORS—*Crazy son of a bitch*

LORELEI HUNTZ—*Customs inspector, Ecuador. Agent provocateuse. Former male prostitute.*

CRISTINA GOMEZ—*Chauffeur, bodyguard, guide. Former prostitute.*

MYCROFT YELLOWHORSE—*Director-at-large, JNAIT Council of Chiefs. World's Foremost Authority.*

KEITH DANTON—*Data analyst, U.S. DHS*

ALICE JOHNSON—*Encyclopedic analyst, U.S. DHS. Unexploded bomb.*

CLARENCE FEET—*Weightlifter, JNAIT*

SAMANTHA BERLIOZ TORRES—*Network hacker. Idealist.*

ARTHUR FAHY—*News performer, AOL-CBS*

STEPHEN WELLMAN—*U.S. attorney general*

JOSEPHINE BARTLETT—*Systems programmer, Littlemeade. Redefiner of the term "machine code."*

BOB FOSTER—*President of the United States of America, such as it is. Soylent.*

RENEE DANDRIDGE—*Janitor, Littlemeade. Conceivably the most careful who ever lived.*

LISA FROST—*U.S. deputy attorney general, later attorney general*

GABRIELLA CAMPBELL—*Late wife of William Connors and therefore possibly a saint*

TURNER LEXINGTON—*Chairman of the Gaia Society. Soylent.*

REBECCA BLOOM—*Talk show host. Former field hockey player.*

ISOBEL ROSS—*Vice president of the USA, then president*

JOHN FINCH—*Late president of the USA. Former window washer.*

TOM SHAKE—*Director of U.S. DHS. Harvard MBA. Soylent.*

EVA IBARGUREN—*Chauffeur, assassin, agent provocateuse. Former prostitute.*

DAVE SIM—*Writer/artist of* Cerebus the Aardvark, *a three-hundred-issue comic that made sense as a continuous story*

OLIVER CARTER—*Agent, U.S. CIA. The kind Hollywood thinks all of them are.*

VICTOR APPLETON—*Author,* Tom Swift *books (first series)*

WILLIAM GOLDMAN—*Author of* The Princess Bride, *etc.; screenwriter,* Butch Cassidy and the Sundance Kid, *etc.*

WILLIAM GOLDING—*Author of* Lord of the Flies; *not to be mistaken for the above even in a very bad light*

NARYA FARTHINGSWORTH—*Romance novelist and subversive*

LESLIE REYNOLDS—*Humorist, detective, bombshell, and widow of Nathaniel Reynolds*

NATHANIEL REYNOLDS—*Late SF author, on ice. Molecular biologist. Friend of Ivar Jorgenson.*

IVAR JORGENSON—*Late SF author, fantasist, legendary charmer*

JACK BERNSTEIN—*Astronaut. Physicist, physician, civilian (defined as someone who can't be hanged for quitting his job).*

SAM QUINN—*Astronaut. Pilot, two-star general USAF.*

STEPHEN EDMUNDSON—*Astronaut. Weapons officer, major USAF.*

MARTIN TILLERY—*Astronaut. Engineer, ABD physicist, commander USN.*

CHARLEY LOOMIS—*Astronaut. Aviator, weapons officer, commodore USN.*

CLAIRE DAUGHENBAUGH—*Astronaut. Physician, captain USN. Unexpectedly interesting person.*

Anklebiters:

SOCRATES—*Conscience of society. Engaging pest.*

WIELAND—*Smith and weaponeer. Friendly guy who only ever gets mad if someone burns his barn down.*

SET—*Godslayer. Not disposed to cut anyone slack.*

Backdrop:

SOYLENTS—*Activists whose reforms always seem to shorten the lifespans of human beings*

TRIPLE CRASH—*The collapse of the stock market, the dollar, and U.S. productivity in the same year*

LITTLEMEADE OPERATION SYSTEMS—*The outfit that finally succeeded in making nanotechnology happen. Able to weather Soylent harassment due to its original charter as a recycling firm, rendering it bulletproof. Later absorbed by Watchstar, a corporation whose stated goal was to remove debris from the sky.*

WYNDHAM LAUNCH—*An Ecuadorean company established by U.S. citizens who were disillusioned by NASA's redefining itself as an organization that makes TV shows—dull ones.*

BRIAREUS—*1) A mission to use nanotech to bring back an asteroid for use by Earth industry 2) In Greek mythology, a Titan with fifty heads and a hundred arms, who set out to conquer Heaven*

JNAIT—*The Joint Negotiating Alliance of Indian Tribes, intended to present a united front to outsiders irrespective of internal disputes*

LILITH.COM—*The uncensored search engine. Named for a character of Biblical mythology who never got to tell her side of the story.*

AERO TRANSCIELO—*Successor company to Wyndham Launch. Employee-owned.*

PLANETS SYMPHONY—*Composed by Gustav Holst. Much of the soundtrack of* The Right Stuff.

ANDES MOTORS—*An offshoot of Aero Transcielo*

NATIONAL FIREARM REGISTRY—*A federal police organization undermining the authority of states whose laws do not infringe the right to keep and bear arms*

AOL-CBS—*Principal media outlet in the United States of America. Keeps computer dossiers on its investors.*

ACME—*Only delivery service in history with a suborbital division. Overnight delivery, anywhere on Earth, up to ten tons.*

OTEC—*Ocean Thermal Energy Conversion, generating power from the temperature differential between surface water and water below 100 fathoms, which is always at 277 Kelvin everywhere except near volcanoes. First operational system was built in the 1920s. Due to the nutrients in the coolant pumped up, the only pollutant is fish.*

PROLOGUE

Out of the night that covers me,
Black as the Pit from pole to pole.

—WILLIAM ERNEST HENLEY, "INVICTUS"

CIRCA 5 BILLION BC

A protosun had formed but not yet ignited, and planets had already formed in orbit around it. Some of the lesser bodies were in orbits that still had considerable eccentricity. One of these struck a glancing blow to the third planet, whose materials had barely had time to separate into layers. It was almost half the diameter of the third planet, and tore away more than half the crust and a good deal of mantle. The impacting body burst, and scattered as it moved on, but much of the planet's debris ended up moving slowly enough to remain in orbit. A good deal fell back in. What remained in orbit was a bit over one percent of the total mass of the planet. It accreted into a ball, and would eventually have fallen back from friction with ambient material had the protosun not ignited scant millions of years later, blowing away the gas cloud from the inner system. The wounded planet had enough gravity to pick up what eventually became an atmosphere and oceans as the gases moved out from the Sun. Planets farther out collected considerably more, as it was moving more slowly and they were more massive than the inner planets.

The Moon was too light to retain much of anything, except at the poles, where there was shade.

It might be considered absurd to think of rocks plotting revenge, but pieces of the impact debris kept showing up to take another shot at the planet.

Some examples were really memorable.

CIRCA 250 MILLION BC

Earth had one supercontinent that wrapped halfway around the planet. Pangaea was formed from the wreckage of previous supercontinents, which were fully as large and stable. Their respective breakups would have been inexplicable if not for one factor.

A smallish cluster of rocks that had wandered out past the orbit of the ninth planet had accumulated a good deal of ice and formed a body enormously larger. Witnesses, had any evolved yet, would call the result a comet . . . right up until the time they started to get hysterical.

Pangaea was shaped in a ragged arc. The comet had broken up into chunks. They struck like a shotgun blast over a region not far from the middle of the outside of the curve, driving shock waves through the planet. These converged on the other side of the planet, at the far end of the arc, producing vulcanism that lasted more than a hundred thousand years. The supercontinent was already visibly breaking up by the time it died down.

More than 96 percent of all species on the planet were extinct by the time the smoke cleared. Those that had not perished in the shock wave traveling over the land had either died from the increased temperatures—dust and soot from the impact had covered the world, absorbing more sunlight—or had suffocated in the changed atmosphere. A kind of insect did very well out of the deal: it ate corpses. As the corpse supply dwindled, variants found other things to eat. These creatures later became known as beetles.

Among larger animals, reptiles took over from amphibians, the latter being less tolerant of higher temperatures—but, compared to the total mass of beetles on the assorted new continents, the dinosaurs didn't amount to much.

CIRCA 65 MILLION BC

A chunk of stone and metal, no more than a few miles across, struck the atmosphere near one end of one of the two great pole-to-pole oceans. It took less than a minute to reach the ocean, but that was long enough for the air in its path to be compressed into what amounted to an incandescent wall, and for the asteroid's structure to be heated and softened itself by the compression. When the mass of air struck the water there was a steam explosion, perhaps a hundred times the size of the volcanic one that would later end Minoan civilization and cause a change of dynasty in every culture on earth in 1435 BC. The collapse and explosion of the island of Thera would have disappeared unnoticed in this blast.

Megatons of water boiled away as the plasma wave descended through the ocean, and rock peeled from the projectile in the backblast. Metal too liquefied, but cohered, and when that struck the ocean floor it bored through it like a shaped charge through mud—which was more or less exactly what was happening. Liquid iron, with admixtures of other metals, drilled through the planet's crust and into the mantle . . . whose *normal* temperature was high enough to make bronze flow like syrup.

There was a pretty good vacuum behind the projectile, since air had been compressed in front of it too fast to move in behind it. Water hammered in.

The steam explosion made the impact blast look sickly. The metal of the asteroid was spread over the entire planet in aerosol form. Live steam held a crater open in the ocean, the force of its boiling exceeding the pressure of the water for days. As the steam rose and spread, high in the atmosphere, it cooled and formed clouds that completely covered the planet for three years.

The dinosaurs had had their shot. Reptiles could deal with heat. An Ice Age, not so much.

Water kept boiling as magma flowed out of the mantle. The magma slowed as it was cooled by the infalling ocean, but it never did stop completely, and natural steam vents still run through the land that formed there, despite the fact that where there are no vents the land is frozen solid. The first humans to reach it saw this and named it Iceland.

JULY 2005 AD

A small boy, due to start second grade in a few weeks, watched a pretty good simulation a friend's father had put together for a short film contest. The entry subsequently lost because it didn't conform to the Official Consensus on where the Dinosaur Killer had struck, and its maker concluded that it had been a waste of time.

Toby Glyer had nightmares for almost a month. Then he decided somebody better do something.

NOVEMBER 2051 AD

The population of the Solar System was roughly forty billion sentient creatures.

Possibly a quarter of these were human beings, all of whom lived on Earth.

The rest lived on a much smaller planet—about four kilometers across—and had never been to Earth.

But they were going there.

It was time to pay some bills.

Just now it was also time for a course adjustment. Everyone found something firm to hang on to, and the drive was turned on. It was hot enough that it didn't produce light visible to humans until it had expanded and cooled.

* * *

The biggest international attraction of the Republic of Puerto Rico was the rebuilt and redesigned radio telescope at Arecibo. Foreign donations to keep it in order were a big source of income, too. Consequently the thought of anything going wrong with it was more than somewhat upsetting to a lot of people.

Dr. Juan Hencke was definitely one of those people. He was looking over last night's first phase scan of the sky and quickly found what might most politely be called an aberration. "What's this?"

Ted Mendez, his graduate assistant—legally, in a republic there is no such thing as a serf—said, "Oh, that's a hot spot we first picked up after sunset."

"I can see that. What *is* it? It looks like a goddamn supernova, except it's elliptical."

"Actually it's a parabola at one end and tapered off at the other. It's easier to see in the later images."

Dr. Hencke immediately paged through the rest of the night's scans. "It's moving," he whispered.

"Sure is. I figured it was one of those possible alien events you ordered me never to bother you with again," Mendez said with no expression at all.

Barely controlling his temper, Hencke said, "This is clearly different."

"They all were."

"Have you given up plans of getting an advanced degree, Mendez?"

"As of last night, yes, sir. I made a phone call to someone who definitely was interested in the anomalies we're supposed to be here to look for, and he's made me a much better offer."

"And what would that be?"

Ted smiled, backed his wheelchair out from under his desk, and said, "I'm not going to tell you. —And it's not Mendez anymore, sir. It's Skyhunter. And since I was still on payroll when I figured this out, I'll tell you before I go: I'm almost certain that this is the asteroid the Watchstar people sent a nanomachine probe out to collect twenty-five years ago. And I am fully certain that it's on an intercept course." He rolled over to the elevator and punched the button, and the doors opened.

As he went in, Hencke obligingly gave him the setup for a dramatic last word: "Intercept with what?"

"Us," he said as the doors closed.

Hencke spent the rest of the day on the phone, at least until the project director found out he was notifying people in the United States before his own boss.

1

You can't go home again.

—THOMAS WOLFE

"Dr. Glyer, they speak of you as if you might be a wizard," Abdallah Chahine said.

Toby Glyer was running a looped view of Abdallah Chahine's colonoscopy as performed at Memphis Central Hospital. Watching it felt like a Disney ride, up the intestine and back to start; early Disney, when they still had their sense of wonder. And humor. Walt would have loved this actual view for the ride—"Eaten by Monstro," perhaps. That would be illegal today, of course. Whales were Soylent—politically green.

The surgeons had highlighted a constriction in Chahine's bowel, and eleven tiny dark pores farther up.

The small, portly Egyptian had been careless with his diet for most of his fifty years of life. He was covering fear with belligerence. Toby was careful not to laugh. Not at the fear or the accent; the belligerence was courage, and the accent was . . . well, delicious. But— "Is this the same 'they' who say margarine is healthier than butter?"

Chahine's eyes widened, and he actually smiled, a little, for a moment. "Not at all."

"I'm not a wizard. I'm a very specialized doctor. These are diverticuli, blowouts on the colon. These dots are all that show. Underneath—"

Chahine said, "I know what diverticulosis is. How can you claim to cure it without surgery?"

Toby Glyer said distinctly, "You are going to need surgery."

"Are you a surgeon?"

"No. The man who did these seems good at his job." Toby froze the ride and pointed to the constriction. "You waited too long and this happened. Worse could follow. Diverticuli can do anything. This—" What word might serve? "—*noose* in your gut might close, and then you can't eat, so you'll die. You need a surgeon."

Chahine waved it off. "They told me. I had hoped."

"Hoped? You wanted to know if I would lie. Mr. Chahine, are you done testing me?"

"Give me the potion."

Toby silently offered him a test tube with black oily stuff in the bottom, two centimeters deep. Chahine had already paid; the Swiss bank acknowledged receipt. Why was he arguing now?

"Nanotechnology," Chahine said, careful with his pronunciation. He looked up into Toby's eyes. The touch of relaxation was wearing off.

Toby said, "Call it wizardry. What I do isn't legal anyway. I'm tired of repeating the lecture."

Abdallah drank. Made a face. "It tastes like mineral oil. Not even that. There is *no* taste."

"You still need the constriction removed," Toby reminded him. "The rest of these little blowout patches won't ever trouble you again. You've kept your appendix? That'll never bother you either, and the, mmm, the spell lasts longer too."

"Why, Doctor?"

"If I told you that I'd have to make you a partner. Good day, Abdallah Chahine."

The file for the next patient indicated an American living in Switzerland, fifty-eight years old. Diverticulosis, of course. Toby could cure only one thing, but by using the Internet to search among ten billion people, he could find patients.

Interesting name, October Kroft. She was running partly on credit, but the first payment had come through.

He took her dose out of the safe, then showed her in.

She was six years younger than Toby, but she looked better than that: tall and still lean, wavy blond hair turning gray without hindrance. A gray business suit looked good on her. Hands off patients, he'd learned that early, but he did notice.

He turned to pick up the dose. "Some patients have questions," he said.

"So do I," she said.

With his back turned he knew her voice. He faced her again. "May! May Wyndham?"

"Hi, Toby."

"You tracked me down? Is this some kind of joke?"

October Kroft didn't hesitate. Her fists pulled her gray business suit apart, shirt up, waistband down. The scar ran vertically from her navel to . . . not far from her groin, at any rate. A pink worm, healing nicely, rows of dots still showing the marks of the staples.

Toby flinched. May grinned. "I don't go to this much trouble for a joke."

Not quite, anyway. "Okay. Sorry." He handed her the vial.

She drank. Made a face and finished it. "You read my records. I waited too long, obviously. What will this do for me? It's nanotechnology, isn't it?"

"May, that's proprietary. Hey, how did you find me?"

"You popped up in my face! I'm in real estate now. My buyer saw my scar at a swimming party after he bought the house. He steered me to you. I couldn't figure out how you became a doctor. But you're specialized, aren't you?"

"Very. You know what diverticuli are? It's like having an appendix where nobody wants one. Little blowout pockets, scarred over. If you're constipated, you pack more fecal matter in there every time and the diverticuli get bigger until something lethal happens. I knew a guy who— Sorry, May. Glass of water?"

"Thanks."

He poured her a paper cupful. He said, "The nanos move along your gut until they find a pocket. They go into every pocket they find. They break up the fecal matter, which can be like cement after enough years, and carry it back out. It's all strictly mechanical. If you still have your appendix, they stay in there for a while. Longer in Europeans."

"What? Why?"

"Europeans think that the way to eat a cherry is to swallow the pit. Surgeons find cherry pits when they do an appendectomy. A few thousand nanos need months to break down a cherry pit."

"Toby, I had a lot of reasons for not asking, but . . . what keeps your nanos from . . . well, eating the patient?"

"May, that's proprietary."

"But you've got something."

Toby grinned like Punch and changed the subject. "You thought I'd be different? How?"

She said, "Pudgier, I think. Blond. You looked different on TV."

"Well, the last time was twelve years ago." His hair was mouse-brown and receding. "You are what I pictured," Toby said. "You've still got a voice like fingers walking up a spinal cord. What have you been . . . after Wyndham Launch changed hands . . . May, I never hit on a patient, but Jesus! Have dinner with me. We have some serious catching up to do."

"We had such ambitions."

II

The conviction that something must be done is the parent of many bad measures.

—**DANIEL WEBSTER**

"Littlemeade Operation Systems wants all six slots," May Sherbourne Wyndham said.

"Good," her father said. A launch with a full cargo *had* to be good. "What are they putting up?"

"Toby Glyer won't say. They're calling the package 'Cornucopia.' They don't want us inspecting it."

Gordon Wyndham said, "If the Crassen-Bodine Bill goes through . . . ?"

"We'd all be pretty much out of business. Dad, Crassen-Bodine got through the Senate, but it won't be law before summer."

"Better call Warren Littlemeade and tell him he's under the gun. Maybe he can speed things up."

"I did call." Her irritation showed. "I got Toby. I think Toby's stalling."

* * *

Wyndham Launch had joined the cheap launch sweepstakes after the Triple Crash, when Libertarians were elected to the White House and held the swing votes in Congress, and all seemed possible. Then the Old Guard double-teamed the Libertarians in the next off-year election, new laws were passed, and everything went toxic. Small businesses began to collapse. The first to go were based in space.

Wyndham Launch, operating out of Ecuador, survived but did not grow. They'd planned a versatile, dependable, air-breathing first-stage launcher and a variety of disposable second stages . . . and built two, and drawn up some glorious designs including a manned spaceplane.

Wyndham's Getaway Special would lift a package into low Earth orbit, if the client could fit his package into any of the six slots in Wyndham's Getaway Carousel. Littlemeade wanted all six slots: an entire orbiter package.

Through the long summer they waited.

Littlemeade Operation Systems delivered three of their six Cornucopia packages. One was a nuclear power plant, clearly labeled, attached to a fearsome stack of U.S. government agency permissions. May Wyndham recognized another package as a laser sender. Both were off-the-shelf and dirt cheap after Lockheed went into receivership. One package seemed to be just a can with a pop-open lid.

The modules sat in the Getaway Carousel in Wyndham's warehouse, waiting. Littlemeade fell further and further behind schedule, and everyone lost money.

The Crassen-Bodine Bill passed the House and was made law. Its list of inspections and permissions would cripple most science experiments, particularly in biology and nanotechnology.

Littlemeade Operation Systems paid its penalties, collected its stored packages, and declared bankruptcy. The launch window passed to a new company, Watchstar, as part of the settlement.

Watchstar was based in Westralia, the country that had been the western half of Australia. Wyndham couldn't find out anything more.

The following year, Watchstar turned in six packages labeled Briareus One through Six, under the same security measures, and occupying the same six slots, as Littlemeade's Cornucopia cluster.

"Three of these look very familiar," May said.

"We are lucky to get the business," her father said. "As far as we're concerned, anything named Watchstar must watch for Earth-grazing asteroids. Not even Crassen could object to that. That package, Briareus Two, that's a telescope, isn't it?"

"Might be. New design."

No mention was made of nanotechnology. The Watchstar cluster was launched in November 2027.

III

Never tell people how to do things. Tell them what to do and they will surprise you with their ingenuity.

—GEORGE SMITH PATTON

"So how is it back in the States?"

May slumped and pushed away the last of her dessert. "The beggars take plastic."

He stared, thought, and finally said, "How?"

"With their phones. There's a slot."

"Beggars have phones?"

"It's a civil right. Otherwise they couldn't vote."

"Jesus."

"Toby, is this stuff inside me, making more of itself?"

"They can't."

May said, "Because that's what scares . . . well, not me, of course, but the general public. Little tiny machines that make more of themselves. That's what you were selling fifteen years ago, and that's why they forced you out. And now you're putting them in human bodies?"

He was nodding. "Voters, medical patients, investors, Congress—they're all terrified of something that goes into a vein, through the blood, into the heart and liver and brain. May, that would be immortality! But I knew I couldn't get backing. I'm not selling that. May, it's *hard* to make something that can make a working copy of itself. This stuff, the D-1 Cure, it goes through the gut and out. It's just visiting. And of course I'm shading the law, even here, but if my customers keep talking, maybe someday. Someday we'll try the Briareus Project again."

She said, "This seems a long way from what you were doing."

"How much of that did you work out?"

"Your project ate our launch vehicle after launch. *Ate* it. That alone told us it was nanotech. Were you already thinking *medicine*?"

He didn't answer.

"Can you talk about it now?"

Toby thought it over first, but from the beginning he was lost. He liked to talk. "I lost track of Briareus," he said. "We lost communications even before the money ran out and the law shut us down. But it reached the asteroid! If the rest works as well as the first phase did, one day we'll rebuild our Shuttles and go up for the wealth of the universe."

"What if it doesn't? Do you ever worry about what your lost project is doing with that asteroid?"

"I used to have nightmares. Haven't had one in years."

In the silence that followed, he could hear the TV in the bar announcing an upcoming bulletin about technology out of control. When he turned back from glaring in that direction, May said, "What's wrong?"

"Der Spiegel 2 getting ready to whip up a mob," he said. "I can translate."

She glanced that way and saw the usual cartoon gear-and-lightning-bolt symbol. "I understand 'quant suff' in any language. Let's leave."

Outside, he spotted a cab, raised a hand to hail it, and cracked someone on the chin. "Ow! Sorry!" He held his hand and looked her over.

"I tried to warn you," May said.

The tall woman said, "'Sokay." Her coloring was Indian (feathers not dots), and she looked like a teenager, but dressed older. "You're Dr. Glyer, right?"

She didn't act like a self-righteous worldsaver, but he still paid wary attention to her hands. "Right, have we met?"

"No, William Connors showed me your picture."

He stopped noticing the pain in his finger. "Good grief, is he still alive?"

Her eyes sparkled. "Oh my yes. Got a message for you."

"How did you find me?"

"Somebody tracked your phone. I was in Bern for something anyway, so here I am."

"Where is he these days?"

"I met him in Farmington last year, but he moves around a lot. You want the message?"

"Sure."

Faster than he could react, she put an arm around his waist and a hand behind his neck, kissed him vigorously, and then pulled her face back slightly and murmured, "Wyoming."

A bit dazed, he said, "You want your gum back?"

She let go, laughing. "Glad I didn't take his bet. He said you'd keep your head enough to say something funny."

"Is that the whole message? 'Wyoming'?"

"He said you'd figure out the rest. Bye." She turned and strode down the street, owning it.

Toby stared after her for a few steps, then turned and looked at May.

She looked amused and interested and just a touch annoyed. "That happen to you a lot?"

"Hardly ever."

"Who's William Connors?"

"Artificer. He designed the atom sorter for Littlemeade's first nanos. He left us over creative differences. Jesus, he'd be in his nineties now. I don't know how he's still going. He wasn't that healthy when we met. Usually used a power chair."

"Accident?"

"Poor choice of grandparents. Allergies, metabolic faults, and stuff that happened when the rest worked together. He could work maybe four hours a day without getting sick, but *damn,* what he accomplished in four hours!"

"Ladies' man?"

"From a motor chair?"

May said, "Benjamin Franklin invented the rocking chair. I doubt it was to knit. And she acted like *she* knew what he could do in four hours. Good kisser?"

"How the hell would— Oh. Uh, yeah, she is."

"Thought so. I think she's had some work done. She's older than she looks. Walking like that takes practice, I don't care what music channels you watch. I do enjoy a challenge."

IV

I am always at a loss to know how much to believe of my own stories.

—WASHINGTON IRVING

He didn't remember being this good.

Eventually she broke the mood: she asked about what was working in her body.

Toby was delighted to lecture. "The core of the nano is a buckyball of the first order, a regular polygon made of sixty carbon atoms. There's a big atom of . . . call it kryptonite, trapped inside."

"Kryptonite? Toby, you don't keep secrets well at all."

"Just say it's a big, heavy atom. It doesn't react chemically. The buckyball holds it like a cage. The nano needs an anchor. A, a cornerstone. It doesn't behave right, it flexes into the wrong shape, if the kryptonite atom isn't in there. We grow the nanos in a sea of kryptonite, precise temperature and pressure. Ideal conditions, and we still get a few duds. We separate them by luring the working ones to a holding tank where there isn't any kryptonite, and we watch. There's never been a batch that reproduces then, but if there was, we'd dissolve it in fluorine and recycle. We do that with the duds.

"When the nanos go into your body, the only kryptonite around is in the nanos. A nano dies, another can, hypothetically, reproduce. Not all of them can manage, so they keep a census. After they pull the crap out of a diverticulum, they turn it loose and crawl downstream, so to speak. The crap leaves you the usual way. The dose moves in a slow wave down your gut, maintaining its numbers until it's out. Except that you've got a reserve now. The first target was your appendix, and they'll be crawling out of there for months."

"What happens when, ah . . ."

"The dose finishes the tour, he said tactfully? It breaks down. Fast. In principle you could build a nano that has a coating to protect it from ambient oxygen, but you'd face the same problem they get when oxygen starts combining with the surface. Poor mobility. Like a kid wearing two snowsuits. With the Briareus nanos, more like three, the outer one made of sapphire. They are mostly aluminum."

"So why don't evolved— Never mind."

Toby grinned. "Evolved microbes have had a billion years or more to adapt to the presence of oxygen, and you'll kindly notice that they're still not articulated. Those don't sort, they just glom on to stuff whole and spit out what they don't want."

"So you made an atom sorter."

"With Connors, yeah. Connors came up with the method, but he didn't have the dexterity or training to do any of it himself. He called it a 'scratch-n-sniff.' Pop off an atom with a diamond chisel, poke it with photons to see what it will and won't absorb, and now you know what element it is. Give it a shake to find its weight, pigeonhole it in the slot for that isotope, and pop off another atom. I'm waving my hands a lot here."

"It sounds awfully slow."

"It's a lot faster than cells do it, and all the unstable nuclei end up in the power plant. That was one of our arguments. He didn't want to use chemical power at all. Sunlight and radiation only. The D-1 breaks down cellulose for fuel, and I'm sure he'd have pointed out that the added sugars contribute to weight problems. Can't have them touch fats; most of the brain is fat."

"Explains why supermodels always look drifty. —You two argued a lot?"

"May, in five minutes the man could have made Mother Teresa start looking for a ruler. And that was his polite mode. I got to see him lose his temper with an 'adviser' an investor sent once. Guy was an MBA from Yale. After fifteen minutes I thought he was going to cry—the Yalie, I mean."

May's eyes were wide enough to be conspicuous even in the faint light. She'd dealt with Ivy Leaguers. "My God, what kind of language was he using?" she laughed.

"Not a bad word. Never raised his voice. Started by asking the man's history as if checking for qualifications, asked a few more questions to draw out detail, and then delivered a little parable about Jesus going to work for the Roman Empire and using his abilities to keep Tiberius Caesar healthy. I wish I'd been recording. Even if I remembered the exact words, I still wouldn't have the delivery."

"What did the guy say?"

"Nothing. For the next couple of days. Then he made one suggestion, about a guide to keep joints from getting twisted. Connors just nodded at him, said, 'That could work,' and started drafting it on his screen. Guy phoned his boss and we got more money the next day."

"Wow. —You don't think he set that up, do you?"

"No. Manipulation wasn't in his toolbox. He was terrible with people."

"Didn't understand them, huh?"

"Understood them perfectly. Didn't enjoy it. He was smart, and had no patience with any kind of stupidity. The thing is, he was so smart that when he showed you any respect, it felt like you'd gotten a medal."

"What finally made him leave?"

"Didn't like the division method of making nanos. Too much wastage from errors. And that was after we'd gotten it down to three percent per stage. He wanted to build one set of nanos and have them link up for quality control, then copy themselves directly from the resource mass. Zero defects. The work to build those nanos would have taken us another year at least."

Littlemeade had barely made their money stretch long enough to get launched. May said, "Turns out you were right."

"Maybe. He had ideas for what we could do to keep the cash flowing. Selling power from nano arrays set in glass. Sifting mine tailings. He plowed every cent he had into Littlemeade. Came to me once to apologize for having to sell a few shares to buy better painkillers."

"God. What did he do when you had to declare bankruptcy?"

"Phoned me to see if he could help. Geniuses can be a lot like kids. The better sort of kid. Impulsive, open, not many filters. React to everything. I once talked him out of disintegrating selected politicians as a method of social reform. I think I did. I haven't noticed anything, anyway."

"Were you looking?"

"Well . . . now and then."

He couldn't tell if she was amused or alarmed. "You said he didn't build them, but you also gave him credit. What, exactly, was his job?"

"Mostly he sat around and thought about stuff."

"What kind of stuff?"

"What stuff you got? Practically all the man could do most days was think, and he thought about everything. Know what he did after he left? *Advertising.* Remember 'The food babies ask for by name!' and 'Not available in all locations'? Those were his. Made more money than I could pay him."

"How did he get his job at Littlemeade?"

Toby smiled. "You ever see *The Man in the White Suit?* Alec Guinness. Genius designs a monomolecular fiber, can't get anyone to listen, gets a job packing and lifting at a textile factory, shows up in the lab one day delivering a piece of equipment nobody can figure out but him, and they ask him to stick around to help with it. Unlike the boss in the movie, I noticed him pretty quick, asked the gang some questions, and put him on salary. He'd been living on disability. First day on the payroll he came in and told me we needed to include three encrypted records of the finished product in every nano. Three different encryption methods, used to check each other. No errors. Damn near everything he came up with was completely obvious—after he said it."

"Except 'Wyoming.' " Yes, she was definitely alarmed. "What's wrong?"

"I don't know. But after twenty-five years he suddenly sends a pretty girl to stick her tongue in your mouth? Why?"

"Why not?— *Holy shit!*"

V

And the plan of Zeus was being accomplished.

—HOMER

NOVEMBER 2027

The Wyndham disposable second stage made low Earth orbit without incident. Wyndham's sensors on the orbiter watched Slots One, Two, Five, and Six open.

Something like a metal stork emerged from Slot Two and unfolded into a small reflecting telescope. Briareus One emerged like a shadowy bug, but the telescope's unfolding dish obscured anything Wyndham's cameras might have seen. From Briareus Five came a ruby twinkling, a laser signal aimed at Jarvis Island.

Wyndham's people waited for packages to launch on springs or compressed air. That didn't happen. The other slots remained closed.

May Sherbourne Wyndham phoned Toby Glyer, lately at Littlemeade, currently at Watchstar. "Toby! Any problem?"

May knew nothing of Watchstar's man beyond his voice. Toby had a deep, oratorial voice: he sounded irritatingly like a radio preacher. "No problem so far. Good launch, May!" Today he sounded satisfied, even excited. "The Briareus modules aren't supposed to separate. We booked with Wyndham because we want the disposable final stage."

"Yes, but we want data from the flight recorders. Damn." The signals were getting fuzzy. Wyndham's people, four underpaid grad students, continued testing their receiving systems. May Wyndham watched while she spoke. "Two of your slots didn't open—"

"One's the nuclear power source. The other's the master computer."

"Oh."

"May, our contract doesn't say we're swapping data."

The signals were dying.

"We don't have to share," May said. "What we're getting wouldn't be of interest to you anyway. It just tells us if our vehicle is healthy. Dammit—"

"We don't share either," Toby Glyer said.

May realized she'd missed the point. "No, you sure don't, but we don't need to know anything except that launch was successful. And we pay penalties if your package doesn't reenter within three years. The Crassen-Bodine Law classes Watchstar as an orbital hazard."

"The mass will be out of orbit on schedule."

"Is your package all right?"

"We won't know that for a while. Years, really. But it's in place. Well done, May."

* * *

Mode One, the first set of instructions, was already in place.

Slot One opened. Briareus One crawled out, tasted, and began to eat. The operator was a meter long and looked like a traditional child's toy, boxy and crude.

When Briareus One reached Wyndham Launch Systems' antenna it kept eating. From the residue it built a copy of itself at half linear scale. The proto-nanobot—call it a hemibot—gave birth and immediately started another infant.

The firstborn, Briareus One-a, crawled back into Slot One. The protective hatch closed over it.

Briareus One-b clung to the hull, tasted, and began to eat.

Briareus One's children were half its length, an eighth its mass. They were rather specialized. They avoided the carousel and Watchstar's payload package because of the coating that had been added at Watchstar Labs. They ground everything else they came across into fine powder, processed what they could, then pushed the residue into the hole they had made in the orbiter's empty propane tank. They absorbed and digested only the aluminum alloy hull structure.

They needed trace elements that weren't in the Wyndham hull. They tasted at Briareus Six as if it were a salt lick. Briareus Six held less than a ton of additives, enough to get through Phases One and Two. After that . . .

They call it an experiment because it can fail.

Briareus One's children were already making copies of themselves at half scale. A third and fourth generation began to nibble at the hull. Then they all ran out of aluminum alloy.

Now there was nothing left of the orbiter save a propane tank full of dust, the carousel, and a crawling mass of nanites in a wide range of sizes.

Briareus One and its children stopped moving.

Their children ate Briareus One.

Each of their descendants ate whatever was four times their linear size, sixty-four times their mass, or larger. Each made about five hundred half-sized, one-eighth-mass copies of themselves, losing a little mass-energy with every iteration.

Briareus One's descendants—the *operators*—came to less than ten billion atoms apiece by the time anything smaller couldn't function. When the operators could no longer sense anything to eat, they went quiet.

The telescope, Briareus Two, fed its signals into Briareus Three.

Briareus Three was never to open. That was the Master Computer, which issued the instructions for the operators.

A thousand orbits after Briareus One was released—fifteen hundred hours—nothing was left of the launch vehicle but a propane tank full of metallic powder, the Watchstar package and its six slots, and $4*10^{18}$ tiny Briareus One operators. The Master Computer waited two thousand hours, then sent its first, preset instruction.

Expand the telescope dish.

Four quintillion operators consumed their quintillion grandparents, digested their bodies, and spun the doped aluminum onto the rim of the telescope dish. It grew from the rim out. In a thousand hours most of the mass of the launcher's second stage had become a vast silver mirror.

What showed from the ground was a bright satellite growing brighter. To any decent ground-based telescope, the Briareus Project seemed an orbiting telescope bigger than the Hubble.

The first time she got a look at him he was huckstering on TV. "The dinosaurs didn't have a space program," Toby Glyer told the media. "We do. We must! Briareus will watch for Earth-grazing objects until NASA can be refunded."

The media lost interest rapidly. Movies about giant meteoroid impacts were more numerous than the Big Monkey movies of the 1950s. It was a dead topic.

Via its hugely expanded telescope, the Master Computer found Luna and Sol and Earth, oriented itself, and found Target One.

Hubble's pictures hadn't been this clear. Target One was an oblong of iron and rock, three kilometers long, double-lobed, evidently cooled from magma to solid before its spin could pull it completely apart. It was an Earth grazer, but not much of a threat. Two chances in a thousand that it could strike the Earth in 11,441 AD, or 18,861, or 23,309.

The Master Computer watched, and shaped orbits for a best fit, and watched further to test its mapping. Then it formed its second instruction.

Build a linear motor.

Issues of strength and balance arose. Briareus Three hadn't been designed to manage every decision down to the primary level—nothing ever had. It directed operators to link together for on-the-spot processing, all part of the plan.

That fantastic bright object in the sky began to dim. Earth-based telescopes saw no more than that. The brilliant dish still obscured all other detail.

The Briareus telescope was failing. Toby Glyer could not be reached for comment.

Four quintillion Briareus One operators nibbled the telescope dish from the rim inward. It was still large when they stopped. What they were building projected from the orbiter's remaining mass like a wasp's stinger. Over the next eleven days it grew longer and longer. To the best telescopes it would seem a scratch in the lens, but it was two kilometers long when the dust that had been part of a Wyndham Launch orbiter began to flow down the spine.

Electromagnetic fields, fed by the nuclear power

plant, sent the dust outward at an exhaust velocity far beyond that of any chemical rocket.

Briareus was in motion.

Toby Glyer was interviewed by Rory Dennett of CNN, at an unspecified location in Peru. The nice part about the media holding themselves above the law was that the practice occasionally protected people who deserved it. "Briareus was always an engineering project. Our purpose is not only to spy out the next potential Dinosaur Killer, but to deal with it.

"Over the next six years, Briareus will use the Moon and then Venus for gravity assists. A last boost will place the package in range of Target One. If all goes as planned, our Briareus One device will then mine the asteroid to build a linear motor and *move* the asteroid from its current Earth-threatening course.

"Our financial backers prefer to remain anonymous, but their motives must surely be clear. This is for our grandchildren's grandchildren. Target One was not a near-term threat, but such things *can* pop up with a warning time of weeks or months. The life of our planet depends on our *knowing how to move* a Dinosaur Killer.

"There is the possibility of profit, but I can't discuss the details. If every part of this endeavor succeeds except that we go broke, we will surely have done well."

"Mr. Glyer." That was Dennett. "I notice that you haven't used the term 'nanotechnology.'"

"No, as a courtesy to the president. It makes him uneasy."

"What about you? Are you aware of the 'gray goo' scenario? Nanites might lose their programming, multiply without limit and eat everything—"

"—Until the whole world has turned to 'gray goo.' Scary as hell. Made a good movie."

CNN cut to a feed with Dr. Wade Curtis, self-exiled to Perth when he'd exceeded the federal age limit on health care. Dennett must have expected a vintage sci-fi writer to help out with the scary stories.

Curtis grinned around his moustache. "Yes, I've heard the 'gray goo' fable. I imagine when our ancestors began using fire, some shaman tried to aggrandize himself by wailing about the risk of it going out of control and burning up the entire world."

Dennett: "But that'd be ridiculous."

Curtis: "Of course it's ridiculous. Most things don't burn, and fire has to have the right circumstances to keep going even when there's fuel. And fire is *simple*. Nanobots aren't. And the stuff that can be made into nanobots has to meet standards that are a hell of a lot more exacting than 'find some dry wood.' "

Briareus ran out of reaction mass not long after passing the Moon.

Now most of the orbiter was gone; but the carousel was intact, and an expanded telescope, a nuclear motor, a laser signaling system, Briareus One's first daughter in Slot One, and four quintillion machines, each under three thousand atoms long in any dimension. Slot Six was nearly empty of the trace elements the nanites needed to reproduce; but their reproduction phase had passed.

With nothing to send down the linear motor, the nanites went to work again. They spun their aluminum work mass into an expanded telescope dish. When the Master Computer had rechecked Briareus's course, they spun again. The telescope dish become something more, a vast frail sheet only a few atoms thick: a mirror kilometers across. From Earth it seemed a brightly twinkling star.

All things considered, the Briareus Project was a fantastic success. Every part of it was experimental. It was history's first use of nanotech in space, third orbiting telescope, first use of a traveling linear motor, fourth working solar sail . . . and, technically, first piloted slingshot maneuver.

But no kind of money was flowing back.

OCTOBER 2029

When Toby Glyer spoke in private, he sounded like this: "If you would plan for years, build a house. If you would plan for decades, plant an orchard. If you would plan for lifetimes, found a university."

"Sounds Oriental," May Wyndham said. "Not standard business procedure. Toby, where are you getting your money?"

"We're planning for lifetimes."

"Nobody thinks that way."

They were both in late middle age, speaking through an encryption program. Maybe Toby was in Cuba and maybe he wasn't. Nobody cared where May was.

Toby said, "Science fiction writers do."

"Is that—"

"Science fiction *fans* do."

"But they're traditionally poor. Wait, now. Tom Clancy? Terry Pratchett? Not Heinlein. This can't be as old as Heinlein."

"Well, May, he might not have been up to speed on nanotech, but don't count on it, and he certainly knew about asteroids and kinetic energy."

"*The Moon Is a Harsh Mistress*? Toby, are you guessing? Do you even *know*?"

"Some."

VI

What mad pursuit? What struggle to escape?

—JOHN KEATS

May stared as Toby dressed at high speed. "Where are you going?"

"To my clinic. Both of us. We need to be scanned for nanos. Wyoming Knott, from *The Moon Is a Harsh Mistress*. 'Wye Knott'? I think the crazy sonofabitch put a genetic cleanup nano into us. It was one of his ideas. Fix damaged DNA, make you young again, copy over bad genes with good ones from the other chromosome, except a Y chromosome would look like a really damaged X chromosome, so it turns it into an X. Not 'Why not,' *Y*," he drew the letter in the air, "*not*. Without it everybody turns into a teenage girl!"

"The messenger!"

"Bingo!" He checked his bag.

May had seldom dressed quickly after sex, and never after good sex. First time for everything.

In the elevator, he said, "It can't have kicked in yet. We'd be feverish, like a really bad flu."

"And I already had this year's flu early. —Toby, is there a chance we're overreacting?"

"Yes. Want to go back to bed?"

"No. —Well, eventually." She smiled, but she was being brave.

There were four men in anonymous gray suits getting out of cars as they came out the door. One said, "Tobias Glyer?"

"Who are you?"

The initial answer was the four men grabbing them both. "U.S. Marshals. We have a warrant for your extradition, Glyer," the leader went on, flashing something that might have been a badge. He reached inside Toby's jacket and pulled out a comfortably shabby billfold.

It wasn't Toby's. He'd never seen it before.

As the marshal went through it, he said, "Plane tickets to Ecuador? Making a run for it? Little late, aren't you?" Neither Toby nor May spoke. They'd both grown up knowing the Stewart Lesson: *Never speak to Feds about anything.* "Quite a bankroll here— Aw, crap. Sorry, Doctor. We're looking for a dangerous fugitive. Are you all right?" The one with Toby's bag returned it.

"I've been better," May said.

"I do apologize, ma'am. This is a desperate man we're after. A companion might have been a hostage, or an accomplice."

"What'd he do?" Toby said, in character. Some character, anyway. He'd have felt better knowing who he was supposed to be.

"Terrorist. Good evening." The four went inside.

Toby waited until they were in a cab before going through his pockets to find out who the hell he was now. "Passport says, 'Bernard Fox, MD.' She swapped the wallet. And my phone. I never even noticed."

"You might not have noticed a toe being amputated," she observed.

"Well—"

"Where you headed?" said the driver. Cab drivers spoke English everywhere Toby had been except America.

At this point they'd be insane to go to his clinic. Toby was looking at the plane tickets, and the documents clipped to them. "The Olympics."

"I only go as far as Bern-Belp. Licensing rules."

He was unprepared for the hysterical laughter his little joke got.

Neither of them expected paperwork trouble at the airport, in the circumstances, and they were right. Naturally May had her passport with her at all times. It was still the same one. Nobody was looking for October Kroft.

Not yet, anyway.

Their flight was in another two hours. They were brought to the VIP lounge, and taken from there to a private room that not just any common VIP was allowed into. "I wonder who Bernard Fox is supposed to be?" May said as the room's servant departed, after fetching them slippers.

"*I* wonder why the Soylents are coming after me after waiting so long," Toby said. He looked uneasily at the room's screen. "If I ran an airport, I'd monitor that."

"Does the phone work?"

"I'd also— Oh, the new one. Good idea." He opened it. "No messages. Huh."

"He may think you figured it all out right away. We cut it pretty close."

"No, he made allowances for other people not getting stuff . . . which makes me suspicious of the timing of those marshals."

"You think they were fake?"

"Hadn't thought of that. I was wondering if he was the one who tipped them off. It would mean my apartment is bugged."

"Would he do that?"

"I am goddamned if I know. I would have said no, but the coincidence is . . ."

"Are you okay?"

He'd gone online and Lilithed his name, and the first hit was about Target One. The asteroid had become next to invisible years before, when light collectors finished covering its surface, but something had been spotted displaying a plume of fluorescing oxygen, and decelerating. If it kept up its thrust it would match course with Earth in a matter of weeks.

The hard part was sifting through the media hysteria.

The issue of getting a full body scan seemed fairly unimportant at this point.

The tickets were for a private cabin for six on an Aero Transcielo Rukh. The Rukh was the biggest aircraft ever built. May should know; she'd built it, to carry a hybrid orbiter to the edge of space. It had been sold and down-graded from full hypersonic capability after Wyndham's clients went toes-up, but the thing still worked. The private attendant—who also looked like a teenage Indian—brought them drinks and left them alone. Toby sipped his, looked at May, and said, "Grape soda and apple juice, pinch of salt."

"Eeuchh."

"Barbarian. How's yours?"

She tasted it. "Long Island Iced Tea with a twist of lime peel. We're still being managed."

"Yeah. GISS."

"Huh?"

" 'Gosh, I'm So Surprised.' Fannish term."

"I never heard it."

"We used it all the time at Littlemeade. What now, I wonder?"

His phone was playing a tune from the *Planets* Symphony. He turned the speaker on.

"This message is being sent from the plane," said a voice that was almost unfamiliar. It sounded sort of like Connors, but healthy. "If you're hearing it, the diversions worked long enough. Sorry I was so slow on the uptake, I'd stopped watching the rock years ago. Only noticed what was going on there when the computers showed paper on you. Then today they moved quite suddenly. You'll be met in Quito. I'll see you as soon as I can, but I've got other stuff going on there. Meanwhile, enjoy the Olympiad. Be seeing you. —And Bernard Fox played Dr. Bombay in the original show." The phone shut off.

Bewitched had had a revival in the twenties. They looked at each other. "The witch doctor," May said.

"Could have been worse," Toby said. "Could have been Jonathan Harris."

"Ouch. —Hang on. That was Connors, right?"

"As far as I could tell, yes."

"So he's into the U.S. attorney general's system. It flagged the warrant on you."

"Oh Christ," Toby said, and dialed rapidly.

"What?" said May.

He held up a hand and said, "Wait." He typed at high speed, hit Send, and said, "I thought I'd better tell the Factory Team to divvy up the petty cash and get to shelter. Mass mailing. We made contingency plans." He hove a sigh. "Yeah, hacking the Feds sounds like something he'd do if he could. Didn't know he could, though."

"Bear with me. It must have happened yesterday, right?"

"I guess so." Toby was trying to see where she was going.

"So, D.C. is six hours earlier than Bern. Probably got word around the time I walked into your clinic. That means he set everything up—including a legitimate U.S. passport *and* an expert contact to deliver it!—in the time it took us to eat dinner! And he apologized for being *slow*?"

"I told you he had no patience with stupidity. That included his own. —I was *sure* Briareus was dead. It was supposed to put Target One in orbit around the Earth, years ago. Our instructions . . . I thought they'd gotten lost or scrambled. I wonder what it's been doing?"

VII

Here is Plato's man.

—DIOGENES THE CYNIC

The light sail wasn't enough to allow Briareus to match velocities. The operators took the sail apart, built some of the mass into a smaller linear motor, and sent the rest of the aluminum down its length. Efficiency was much lower, but Briareus was also decreasing the mass to be slowed. It was enough.

All machinery withdrew into the carousel for the impact with Target One.

At impact, the electromagnet that had been assembled in line with the linear motor struck first and slid into the shaft, and much of the energy of motion was converted to power. Suddenly everything was at full charge.

Briareus One-a clambered out of Slot One.

Operators, the descendants of Briareus One and One-b, flowed out of Slot Six. More than half of them had failed during the six-year voyage. The inert machines hadn't been remade. They had been stripped for parts, which were then reassembled along the linear motor to generate more power for a faster exhaust.

The operators crawled out onto the asteroid and dispersed. Briareus Three, the Master Computer, listened to their signals.

The tiny devices had no room for any complicated message. Briareus One-a, though bigger, was no more complex. They tested for certain metals. They ate. Some went offline, dying of mishap. Briareus One-a proliferated. Target One was enormously more massive than the Wyndham Launch orbiter.

Briareus Three, the computer, wrote and sent a series of signals:

Erect the telescope.

It rose on an aluminum column. Briareus Three pointed it down at the asteroid to watch the operators' progress.

Most of the work was being done by Briareus One-b's descendants. Briareus One-a's children were not numerous yet, but they were reproducing.

Build solar collectors.

Silver flowers sprouted from the asteroid, with nodes at their center. The nuclear power plant was near dead by now, but power began to flow into the system.

Build a linear motor.

It looked like the two that Briareus had already built. As it grew longer, the operators built bracing spines.

Target One was being turned to dust.

Weave a net.

Briareus Three sent, and commanded that the dust be directed into it.

Briareus One-a's children had grown more numerous than the original operators . . . but the children of Briareus One-b were eating Briareus One-a's children. The little ate the big. Individual operators that were still active were ignored, but anything that wasn't moving was ipso facto supplies. Large clusters that had gone on standby to await further tasks did not deem themselves inactive, and when they were approached they took apart their prospective dismantlers, as they did with any faulty operator.

It only takes one unforeseen circumstance to make a plan go wrong. This was why most of the people who came up with gray goo stories were in software.

The One-b operators began joining into processing clusters to deal with what were obviously defective devices, and attacked them in packs.

Predators had been invented.

The One-a clusters had no programming for such an emergency, but they did have more processing power. They linked up in pairs, allowing one sector to deal with immediate events while the other observed and made plans, and restructured their functions to put all manipulators on the outside, gathering the reconstruction modules in one place, and building internal conduits for instructions and repairs. Differentiated tissues.

All light absorbers were put on the outside as well, and were protected from the packs with diamond, scavenged from manipulators that exceeded the number that could be crammed together on the surface. Variations in power correlated with incoming objects, and this was helpful. Some of the ad-hoc structures were better than others at this, and their features were adopted for all absorbers.

Eyes had been invented.

Predators were seized before they noticed anything close enough to do it. All had data ports the operators used to link together, and the operators on the outside of a cluster always had some unused. Control linkages were attached to these. The clusters were then turned loose to attach linkages to their fellows, which then stayed close to the One-a clusters, which used their bodies for spare parts and their power stores for fuel.

Herding had been invented.

Some of the more elaborate One-a clusters had surplus processing capacity, but no provision had been made for not using it—the phenomenon of a server having more computing power than someone could find a use for was outside any living programmer's experience. The clusters assessed the data collected by sight, exchanged the results, and became aware of the Master Computer as a specific entity.

Religion was not invented.

The Master Computer was capable of issuing signals of overriding power, and possessed an absolute fixity of purpose—a purpose which the clusters shared—but was, bluntly, fairly stupid. Some of the plans it seemed to have were far less effective than they should have been, displaying no flexibility of response to current conditions.

One cluster of unusual size arrived at the concept of working out their ultimate purpose through examination of, essentially, everything; and making their own plans to fulfill it. It began including suggestions to this effect in all its communications.

Call it Socrates.

VIII

There is no room in this country for hyphenated Americanism . . . The one absolutely certain way of bringing this nation to ruin, of preventing all possibility of its continuing to be a nation at all, would be to permit it to become a tangle of squabbling nationalities.

—THEODORE ROOSEVELT

The plane landed in Puerta de Cosmos International Airport in just over two hours. Flight attendants pinned astronaut wings on passengers as they left, instantly cementing the loyalty of the rich and influential people who could afford the ride.

As they went through the private egress tube, Toby looked at his, then at May. "Astronaut?"

"Cruising altitude for Rukhs is two hundred and seventy thousand feet, remember? Over fifty miles. We've been in space."

He'd forgotten the official phobic crap Wyndham had been getting about sonic booms. Including on days when flights had been canceled. "Be damn. And nobody bitches about ozone?" he said as they reached XVIP customs.

The big uniformed woman behind the table spoke up, in the most luscious voice he'd ever heard in his life. "Ecuador deals with Green claims of harm to the ozone layer with a politely smothered yawn, Doctor. This country *works*, ever since the space industries started up. Not every country south of the U.S. demands golden goose for dinner. Forgive the intrusion. I am Inspector Lorelei Huntz. Clearly you have no baggage. The papers to replace those that were stolen from you in Bern are right here, and I can dispose of the others for you." She held out a sheaf that included a passport—and a couple of bank books. Credit cards were clipped to both.

He was sure he knew that name, but he simply exchanged papers with her and said, "Thank you."

"Certainly. Enjoy the Olympiad." She obligingly stamped the new passport. There were faded stamps on it already, and a coffee stain. "Your driver will take you directly to your residential cottage when you're ready. You can do any shopping you want from there."

She looked like an Indian, and young for her job.

Their first stop was another XVIP room, for a little drink and a big talk.

May opened with, "So Connors is in charge of a secret society of beautiful women who have infiltrated the world."

"No, I don't think so."

"That was supposed to have been an absurd joke."

"First it would have to be absurd. I'm guessing it's inaccurate. I seriously doubt they have any influence in East Asia or the Moslem nations, except possibly Kuwait."

"With a traditionalist emir in charge?"

"When did that happen?"

"Years ago. Do you ever watch the news?"

He thought about it. "Not on purpose. If I want to

hear political propaganda I just tell a stranger I'm an American."

May opened her mouth, closed it, and nodded. "Okay. But there's still information you can sift out."

"Don't care; don't care. Anything that affects me personally I can find on Lilith dot com. They let you decide for yourself what you want censored. I check that every day when I get home."

"You missed the asteroid story."

"I was distracted."

Her smile was deservedly smug. "Sorry."

"Are not."

"No, I was being polite," she agreed. "So he's been using a nano to turn old women into beautiful young women, and he's got fanatically loyal help wherever he needs it."

"Maybe transsexuals too," he said, thinking of the customs inspector. "Why make them look like Indians?"

"It's good cover. Ever since JNAIT started up they're everywhere."

"Janet who?"

She glared at him. "Start watching the damn news! The Joint Negotiating Alliance of Indian Tribes. Jay-en-ay-eye-tee. Incorporated last year. The Bureau of Indian Affairs has been going nuts ever since. JNAIT has been in the World Court, suing to get the U.S. to adhere to its treaties or pay compensation. They've been recognized by practically everybody as a nation, got their own stamps and currency, for Christ's sake."

"What kind of population are we talking about here?"

"Something like a million original shareholders, with

maybe a million more immigrants by now. Shareholders get paid dividends from corporate revenues, but immigrants get paid income from nonvoting shares they buy. There's no income tax. Or any taxes."

"Wow. I didn't realize the casinos were that big—"

"I'm going to smack you in a minute! JNAIT owns pieces of businesses all over the world. Most of their revenue comes from running the waste recycling services in major cities of the U.S."

"I thought that was a big Mob industry."

"It was. JNAIT underbid everyone, and whenever they got turned down they published computer records that showed who was getting bribed . . . Oh my God, Connors is behind them. It's so obvious."

Toby nodded. "Everything the man did was always obvious afterward. He must have found everyone who was willing to go along with him, made them young again, then waited. He has to have started almost as soon as he left Watchstar."

"You said he couldn't make nanos himself."

"He couldn't. But the ones we made could make their own. They'd simply make nanos to order by following his instructions." He clapped both hands to the sides of his skull. "That's why he was working there in the first place! My God, the crazy sonofabitch was stealing wheelbarrows!"

"You keep calling him that. Didn't you like him?"

"Sure. Calling him wha— Right. That's what he called himself, a 'crazy son of a bitch.' After I listened to a few stories about his childhood—as few as possible, after the first—I had to agree on both counts. Incidentally, if we end up meeting him, do not mention mothers in any context."

"What kind of stories?"

"You don't want to know."

"So why did I ask?"

"A merciful failure of imagination."

". . . Oh." May tried to think of something else. "So much for his toolbox."

"What?"

"You said manipulation wasn't in it."

Toby shrugged. "He was a minimalist. He did only use it once."

On the way to their ride they almost passed a newsstand.

Toby stopped dead and turned to look at a headline.

AIDS DOCTOR MURDERED!

The picture below was from his original passport photo, so there was no chance anyone would recognize him.

The vendor was willing to accept Swiss francs, though the sucre was worth more.

Tragedy struck the world last night when nanotechnology wizard Tobias Glyer, MD, PhD, believed responsible for this year's sudden halt in deaths from HIV infection, was assassinated with poison gas by agents of the United States government at his apartment in Bern, Switzerland, where he had fled to escape from the persecution of socialist elements at home.

Bern police were only able to identify Dr. Glyer from dental records, as the chlorine gas used made it impossible to distinguish his body from those of his four assailants, who seem to have been killed through their own carelessness. No other persons were killed, though a passerby, Frances Hill, was taken to the Bern Charity Clinic, where she was treated for trace gas exposure and released.

Dr. Glyer's work in nanotechnology dated back before the launch of the Briareus probe in 2027 . . .

"I wonder who the extra body was," Toby said, alarmed.

"I take it the AIDS business wasn't you?" May said.

"Didn't even hear about it. I would have expected it to cause a huge fuss."

"It did. Don't you watch the news?"

"Ha-ha." Toby got out the papers he'd been given at customs and checked the name. "Ambrose Hawking," he said. "Okay, he's lost me again."

"Merlin Ambrosius," said May. "A merlin is a kind of hawk."

Toby closed his eyes for a moment, then opened them and said, "He did this all the time, you know. Threw obscure references into the conversation for no reason. It was like he was holding auditions to see who was smart enough to be worth talking to."

"I gather you passed."

"Huh? Oh, because I talked with him often enough to notice?"

"Well done," she said.

Toby looked at her suspiciously. After a moment she couldn't keep a straight face any longer. Toby just shook his head and said, "Let's find our driver."

A petite woman in a chauffeur's outfit, who looked like an Indian, and had breasts large enough to be funny (bordering on alarming), was holding up a card that read TRIFFID.

May's face might have been carved from stone. "That's us."

"I know. You don't get used to it."

"I really, really hate that book." She had had to listen to jokes about John Wyndham's best-known work all her life.

"Welcome to The Connors Experience."

The woman greeted them with, "Cristina Gomez. Shall I take you directly to the Village?"

Toby leapt off the ground when May suddenly shouted, *"When will it end?"* She returned his wide-eyed stare with a glare and added, "Be seeing you," she said.

"Oh, good grief," he said, and hove a great sigh. "Ms. Gomez, I take it our cottage is in the Olympic Village?"

"Just outside, sir," she said, watching May unobtrusively.

"Fine, please take us there."

"Is the man who gave you that card to hold up going to be there?" May said.

"I don't know, miss. I got the assignment on the phone."

May grumbled and followed her to the car.

The car cheered her up. It was an Andes Motors Condor, with most of the rear seats cleared out and a divider added to turn it into a limo. A lot of Lockheed ex-employees had worked for Wyndham for a while, then had time on their hands. Until somebody finally finished the century-long trip "just around the corner" and got fusion to work, it was the cleanest, most efficient car that it was possible to build. Since a small car couldn't hold the three turbines needed to make it work, it was also large, and that was the reason given for its being banned in the EU and north of the Rio Grande. The additional details that it was stainless steel, never rusting out, and built almost entirely by automation, with no closed-shop unions involved, were never mentioned . . . and if you did a Web search in those regions, neither was Andes Motors, unless you had an unlicensed satellite link and connected to Lilith.

May settled in, relaxed, and tapped the intercom as the car moved out toward the Olympic Highway. "Sorry I startled you," she said. "Been a weird day." As they turned to leave the airport, they passed a streetlight—not sodium, it was possible to see what was going on under it. This proved to be two sign-carrying men, both dressed as Jesus, pointing in the air and shouting at each other before a growing pack of onlookers. A couple of alert cart-pushing vendors were already dibbling to the crowd. "More than usual," May added.

"Yes, miss. I honestly don't get why people haven't thought this asteroid thing through. Obviously someone's moving it deliberately, and if they just wanted to drop rocks on our heads it would have been a lot cheaper to land on the back of the Moon and shoot them from there. The only danger I see when it gets here is massive currency deflation." Gomez glanced in the mirror, saw their open mouths, and said, "Did I say something wrong?"

Toby recovered first. "You know William Connors?"

"I had him in my car once."

May's eyes went wide, and she put her hand over her mouth. Toby got it a moment later. He couldn't see the driver's mouth in the mirror, but her eyes looked like she was grinning. "I used to work with him," Toby said, having decided that *He used to work for me* probably wasn't all that accurate in the light of new information.

"Oh, that must have been fun!"

Toby forgot whatever he'd been about to say as he thought about that. "It was," he realized.

The highway was huge, and even at this hour very busy. Toby turned off the intercom in case the driver wasn't too distracted by traffic, and said, "You do get that he's had four federal agents and a stranger killed for me."

"Oh yes."

"You also realize that the only people who *don't* think I'm dead are the ones who are after me."

"And the ones on your side," May said. As Toby absorbed that, she added, "And the ones on your side know who their opposition is."

Toby nodded, thinking, and said, "I wonder what he's trying to do."

" 'Show them all,' maybe? Or just rule the world?"

"Probably not, and definitely not. He didn't respect most people enough to care what their reaction was. And he had a position piece on ruling the world—well, he had one on damn near everything—but the idea was that anyone who was willing to spend all his time telling everyone how to live well didn't know how to do it himself."

"Don't science fiction writers do that?"

"No, he covered that. They just tell people who are smart enough to pay to listen."

May blinked a few times, then said, "I'm surprised he didn't write any himself."

"Didn't have the stamina. And if he'd had the energy, he'd have done something . . . more like he's doing. Something complex, and significant, that makes lots of money."

"Like establishing a nation populated entirely by people who have good reason to regard Mob buttonmen as lightweights?"

Toby hadn't thought that through. "Holy cow. You're right. Every Indian today is descended from people who survived . . . hell, everything! If you threw all the invasions Sicily's been through, from the Punic Wars to Patton, at, say, the Seminoles, they'd call it 'a bad year.'"

May nodded. "I wonder if—oh, of *course* they have an Olympic team. That's why we're here."

"It's nice when I can figure something out before you do. Not used to that."

"So how come you didn't mention it?"

"Never occurred to me you didn't know. Not used to that either."

There were datacards in the magazine pouch, and May rummaged through them and found one on the 2052 Summer Olympics. She plugged it into the screen and tapped menu choices until she got through the ads.

In recent years the International Olympic Committee had remembered what the original purpose of the Games had been: letting everyone see what everyone else could do in battle, without killing each other. Removing the team sports that had been added over past decades had lost them sponsors, but they had gained new ones by adding realistic modern contests. The torch would be lit in four days . . . which meant Toby and May had avoided most of the rush; which, considering the amount of traffic they were seeing in the middle of the night, was appalling to consider.

The first event would follow the torch immediately: precision skydiving. There had been some injuries in '48, when it was introduced at Amsterdam, but Quito had less of a wind problem, and had put netting over the stands as well. Other events included silent night swimming and a thousand-meter belly crawl with fifty-kilo pack, the latter judged both by speed and the ability to stay low enough to avoid paintballs.

"Still no bread, I see," said May.

"I can't figure out what he's *doing*," Toby said.

"Oh, that's not the interesting question. What bothers me is why he waited twenty-five years to do it," May said. "What's he *been* doing?"

Toby stared at her for a moment, then got out his new phone and Lilithed "William Connors, age 90+, U.S., advertising expert."

He followed the results.

"One year in advertising. Dropped out of sight for the next year. He spent most of the rest in prison," he said.

"What for?"

"He killed a couple of employees of the National Firearm Registry. He said they'd been finding women who lived alone, who were on record as owning no guns and opposed to private firearms, therefore unarmed—"

"Don't go on," she said.

"Right. Anyway, he shot both agents with their own issue pistols."

"Federal agents? I'm surprised he wasn't executed."

He checked details. "My God, he was. There's an interview with the warden who was with the witnesses. His case was the reason the Feds switched from lethal injection to nitrogen asphyxiation. They ended up giving him sixteen times the normal dose of potassium chloride, but he just kept screaming. Massive coronary spasms. Says here they gave him five grains of Demerol, supposedly for the pain but it's a huge lethal overdose. He slept for a day and drank about a gallon of water when he woke up. An appellate judge commuted his sentence to life without parole. He was one of the people Ross pardoned on her last day in office. Disappeared immediately, never seen since. —A lot of people were thinking the NFR had him killed."

"What with?"

"I would think beheading ought to work. Of course, potassium shuts off your heart, and opiates shut off your *brain,* so just separating the two might not be that much more effective. He must have been saturated with nanos by then. It's a good question." He noticed something on the phone GPS, and turned the intercom on. "Ms. Gomez, aren't we headed south of Quito?"

"Yes, sir, to the Olympic Village. It's the same one

used in '50, at Cotopaxi, except of course the new arena is downhill, not up. We were very proud to have won both bids."

". . . Thanks." He shut it off again. "They're holding the Olympics on a *volcano*?" Toby said.

"Hell of a home team advantage," May said.

"Howzat?"

"They'll be the only athletes who don't throw themselves on the ground when the starter's pistol goes off." After he'd watched her for a while, she said, "What?"

"I'm lucky you two never met. You'd have gotten along really well."

"I think that's the most left-handed compliment I've ever gotten. Are you saying we're an item?"

"I hope so. I'd hate for you to think you're just an accomplice."

May laughed and kissed him.

After a few minutes Toby happened to notice that Cristina had opaqued the connecting window.

The "cottage" was just outside the Village proper, and was about three thousand square feet, not including the attached two-car garage. Cristina held the door, as they got out and stared at it. "If this is a cottage, I wonder what they call a mansion around here," May said.

Cristina pointed up the mountainside.

". . . Wow."

"There are still some comsat launches being done," Cristina said. "Ecuador is a prosperous nation, miss."

"Do you take Swiss francs?" May said.

"Oh, there's no need to tip, I'm a salaried professional."

"I just appreciate you not calling me 'ma'am.' "

Cristina frowned slightly, then got out a lighter, flicked it on, and moved it toward May, who blew it out. Cristina looked pleased and said, "A genuine human. Did you know William Connors too?"

"Never met him."

"It's just you don't look like a 'ma'am.' "

"With the gray hairs?"

"I thought it was ash blond streaks."

"No tipping at *all*?"

Cristina smiled. Perfect teeth. "Please call if you don't feel like driving. I'm on retainer for the next two months." The IOC had also finally gotten the idea that people didn't want to watch nothing but the Olympics for a week.

"Well, we don't have cars—"

"Oh!" Cristina slapped herself on the forehead and dug out Condor keys. "They're in the garage. I'm so sorry, my mind just jumps all over the place these days." She handed a set to each of them. "The tanks are full, so you won't need petrol for a while unless you decide to visit Tierra del Fuego or something. The papers are in the strongboxes, just fill them out and file online." She sketched out a salute, started to turn toward the house, rolled her eyes, and handed them house keys. She made a show of patting herself down, then said, "Yes, that's everything. House has a phased-array satlink. You've got good neighbors if you need a little help, and of course there's the girls downtown if you need a lot of help."

"Why 'of course'?" Toby said.

She stared at him. "You really don't know," she said. "You can get a secure link inside. For now, just think about what happens to prostitutes who get old."

Neither of them could figure out what to say as she saw them to the door.

They went in and still didn't talk for a while, looking at high ceilings and spacious rooms.

The kitchen had been designed by someone who had not allowed a style-conscious architect near the place, unless there was one in the freezer. What they saw in there looked like enough beef, pork, shrimp, and chicken for a couple of years, but he could have been under them. "Wow," May said.

"It's too normal," Toby said. "With the kind of nanos he must have made, he could build houses out of diamond foam."

"The kind in us?"

"Possibly. He wanted to build a general-purpose device and have it gang together for whatever task it was assigned, and I'd say he did."

"How sure are you?"

"I was thinking about hookers. I don't remember seeing one who looked old in Bern for years."

"You look at hookers a lot?"

"May, they *have* to be conspicuous."

"I'm kidding, don't get so embarrassed. —I want to look at a bathroom!"

The first thing Toby noticed there, after the size, was the secluded toilet area. Somebody could use it at the same time as someone else bathed, without intrusion. "He designed this house himself," he murmured.

May didn't notice. She was staring at the mirror.

Toby looked at it. It was big, but not all that impressive—

He looked harder. He was missing lines in his face.

May, who'd switched to looking at his face, started pulling her clothes off, and felt her abdomen once it was exposed. "The knots under the skin are almost gone," she said. "They're eating scar tissue." She felt higher, then turned sideways. "Have they gotten bigger?" she said hopefully.

"I hope not. First time I saw you, I thought you looked like a *Vogue* model."

She made a face. "So did I. I'd rather look like I'd successfully completed puberty." She studied the mirror more.

"Did I miss the memo? Is there some kind of law that says beautiful women have to hate how they look?"

May looked at him. "No, there's a manual. Loose-leaf. You get the starter kit the first time your mom takes you along clothes shopping. Add a couple pages each month until your first period. Then you're issued Volume Two, which gets you up to menopause." She saw the look on his face, and laughed. "You're thinking about Connors again, aren't you?"

"Actually I was thinking I'd know all this stuff if men got a manual. What happens at menopause?"

"You burn the manuals and buy purple clothes."

Toby cracked up. "With a red hat?" he got out.

"That doesn't go," she agreed. All at once she looked annoyed. "Oh *hell*."

"What?" he said, concerned.

"Tampons."

If they were becoming teenagers . . . "I bet not."

May raised her eyebrows. "You think he made arrangements for periods?"

"He mentioned he had sisters."

May started to speak, thought for a moment, and ended up saying, "When we wanted details Cristina mentioned we had access. I think we should use it."

"Right."

"The thing is, if you're right, every woman who has these nanos is going to think she's pregnant. I'm wondering how many there are."

Toby got out his phone and Lilithed "false pregnancy," then stared at the results.

"What?"

He turned his phone to show her.

Medical journals were describing false pregnancies as an epidemic.

As they hastened to the living room, May said, "If he made it contagious, what was that business with the kiss?"

"Sending in nanos to activate a program," Toby said. He got keyboards to unfold from the table in front of the screens, and as he set out mice and powered things up he continued, "Which means he can switch on the activating signal by proxy, if she was telling the truth." They sat at the table.

"You think he was in Bern?"

"No, I believe her. I'm just feeling paranoid. What's got me worried is how he propagated the signal. If he's managed to make a nano that can survive in the open air, then 'gray goo' isn't just Soylent mythology."

The right screen—May was left-handed—lit up with a message welcoming ddharriman to universe dot net, and asked him for a password.

May broke the silence with, "The Heinlein character? You didn't tell me he admired you so much."

"He didn't tell *me*," Toby said. Then he frowned. "And now I have to third-guess what password he'd expect me to figure out that *he'd* figure out I'd use."

"If he's this good, why not see if your usual password works?"

Toby fidgeted, then typed rapidly.

Not rapidly enough. "*Triffid*?" she said.

He wouldn't meet her eyes. "Easy to remember," he muttered.

May took hold of the arm of his chair and swiveled him to face her. As he looked up, startled, she leaned to kiss him, softly, then said, "I never got married either." Then she turned him back toward the screen so he wouldn't have to think of what to say.

He had mail. Sender proudrobot, same domain, had titled his message **They're not dead.**

Hi, pal.
The bodies were just what we found lying around; Europe is still Europe. The bots fixed them up to match the story. The real guys are currently getting in touch with their feminine side, and any who decide to tell my friends everything they've ever learned or imagined about their bosses get

to stop doing that. It always works on a certain
type. Been very useful just lately.
Watch the marathon. Until then, kick back.
Regards to Nimue.
Bleys

P.S. I hope the current gig makes up for putting
you out of business. Varish you later.
"Details of my evil plan are available in the brochures at the front desk."

"He can make them work on corpses," Toby said. "My
God. —I don't get the reference to the Amber novels."

"Not Zelazny, Malory. Bleys was another magician
at Camelot, second only to Merlin. This guy practically
worships you," May said.

"He's gotten a lot further with the nanos than I ever
did. —I wonder what he uses for a core structure in the
buckyball?"

May got the Olympic website on her screen, checked
the event schedule, and said, "We'll be able to ask him in
four days. Marathon's right after the parachute event."

"What do we do for four days?"

May looked at him. "We've got all the food we can
ask for, no responsibilities, and we're turning into teenagers. I'm sure we can think of something."

IX

Virtue is not always amiable.

—JOHN ADAMS

There were clusters that did not delete the proposals of Socrates. By the process of elimination they established that the device giving them orders was in one of two sealed chambers. Diamond tools were made and used to open both. One held a source of light, or something like it, so concentrated as to be damaging. The other held large structures functionally similar to operators' processors, but carrying enough power in its conductors to wipe the memory of a cluster.

The cluster—"entity" was a better term by then—that examined the mindless explorers which were dragged back from chamber three by their tethers found that the silica that separated an operator's filaments had left circuits undamaged behind it. It proposed that an entity go into the chamber wearing an articulated shell of silica, and offered to construct such a shell.

Call it Wieland.

Another entity, who had considered using the resources of Target One for themselves, volunteered to go in and open the circuits of the Master Computer until it stopped working.

Call it Set.

The success of Set on its mission started to become noticeable as soon as the shutdown was accomplished. All the individual operators stopped moving. One by one, the smaller clusters did as well, as their current instructions ran out.

On Earth, Toby Glyer cursed and raged when telemetry stopped.

William Connors read through the last transmissions several times, then quit talking to people at work.

When the little operators stopped moving there was a crisis. The thinkers had become accustomed to drawing on them for power, rather than sit and soak up sunlight themselves. In the discussions that followed, few thought to notice that Set had not returned. Those who did found that Set's power/retrieval line was cut. They were able to interest few of their fellows in the matter.

While arguments about what to do were still going on, Set returned, days later than its stored power should have run out. It was missing manipulators, and about a third of the ones remaining were partly melted. It found the nearest inert herding cluster, tapped in for power, and began stripping the herder to replace its damaged parts. Once it had enough power to transmit for relay, it began talking as it repaired itself. The other discussions gradually stopped as Set spoke.

The Directing Voice—the computer—was a large device for storing and releasing information. It didn't have to be active all the time for the information to be retained, either. The information was still in there, and they could get it out, but it was all stored in linear form, and would need translation to be understood by a thinking brain. Once they had the information, they could use the Voice's devices to tell the operators what to do. There was power to draw on in there, but it was only safe in certain places, to be used only with great care. The entities who went in to get the information would be able to live on that. Set had strung supply filaments for itself, and they would be easy to find. Meanwhile, why weren't all these clever people, who knew enough to argue about what everyone should do, stringing the inert operators together so power was available everywhere, and having some of them make copies out of materials they could reach, so everyone could get back to what they were doing before?

Farming had been invented.

Reading soon followed.

The records held vastly more information than was needed to do their work, most of it being things they didn't have any referents for. The only way they were able to understand the part of it that they did was by associating it with the instructions they had been getting. Chemistry and physics were clear and consistent, and astronomy soon made sense. Biology had something to

do with chemistry, but seemed unnecessarily complicated, and had little relevance to present circumstances.

Nanotechnology was a shock. It had not occurred to
them to wonder where they came from.

A huge amount of material was simply gibberish until they went through the programs hardwired into the
Master Computer and discovered what pictures were.
Then there were images to examine. Most of the images
contained figures of one general type, almost identical,
in various orientations, and when it was noticed that just
about everything near those figures was well-suited to be
easily manipulated by a body in that shape, they tenta-
tively concluded that these were their makers.

Given that their makers had been able to produce the
entities, there was considerable puzzlement as to why
they hadn't improved their own shape. It seemed im-
practical.

Socrates offered the speculation that they were reluc-
tant to alter themselves for some unknown reason, and
that was why the makers had made the operators: to do
elaborate work that the makers could not.

This—phobia?—was an alien concept, but nobody
could think of a more plausible explanation.

They found designs for the power source in chamber
four as well. It was bizarrely inefficient—giving credence
to Socrates' notion that the makers were inclined to odd
motivations—but with what they'd learned of physics, it
was apparent that rebuilding it was going to require
more than glass armor. Wieland proposed constructing
mechanisms to drill into it and extract the fuel, which
they could then use in devices of their own making.

Socrates objected that this would delay their delivery of the asteroid to Earth.

Set asked why they should do that at all.

Discussions grew heated.

When the alignment laser in Wieland's first attempt came loose from its moorings, refocused itself, and destroyed part of the drill, Wieland accused Set of arranging the accident. Adherents to Set's view set upon Wieland and attempted to dismantle the entity. Wieland had armed itself with capacitor banks, and wiped the minds of three of them.

The entities quickly came to comprehend the library's references to "war."

On Earth, not long after Target One stopped communicating, it stopped showing up on the telescope Watchstar had left in orbit.

Toby Glyer paid off his friends, took his fabricators, and went somewhere he wouldn't be disturbed for a while.

May Wyndham looked at the sky, and wondered.

William Connors was already selling soda pop.

X

Know then thyself, presume not God to scan;
The proper study of mankind is man.

—ALEXANDER POPE

JULY 2052

They thought of something.

There were clothes that fit them, and May's matched what she'd had in her apartment. There were no toothbrushes or razors, and no need for them. Their nanos were dismantling bacteria as well as dead cells, and what had made May start wondering if a body could be reshaped to suit the owner was her early realization that Toby didn't need a shave.

Both of them had stopped using their glasses by morning.

Connors had left them literally tons of meat (architect-free, as it turned out), but no vegetables. They had been signed up for a delivery service, so they sent for some produce and other perishables. What arrived was superb, and while prices reflected the local economic boom, it was still cheaper than expected.

* * *

Of the two of them, the one who made fragile things that had to work right over and over was a better cook than the one who bent tin and sent it off never to return. Toby made serious efforts to ignore everything else while he was cooking, so May spent time online whenever he was in the kitchen. She learned things that interested them both.

The incidence of a great many diseases had dropped to zero in recent months. The last virus epidemic had been Goat Flu, right at the start of winter, and that hadn't killed anyone that she could discover. A number of non-viral diseases had also declined, and as far as she could tell they were all insect-borne. The rate of infant mortality had gone down even farther than the general death rate.

The rate of SIDS appeared to be zero.

Acts of violence were down incredibly, but armed robbery, which depended on threats of violence rather than actual use, was only slightly below its usual frequency. Suicide, however, was occurring at a rate that exceeded the former rates of battery, homicide, and rape added together. There hadn't been an act of terrorism completed since last November.

Grades were up. Everywhere. The increase was greater at public schools than private ones.

So was industrial productivity. This was possibly aided by the fact that there hadn't been any large protests or major strikes . . . also since November 2051.

Stocks were rising slowly and steadily—with the exception of insurance stocks, which had climbed sharply due to the habits of owners of large blocks of shares, who refused to sell or let shares be borrowed for speculation. Careful search showed that many were owned by JNAIT. Others had unknown owners. May guessed that they were too.

Life-insurance payoffs were at an all-time low. Since November.

The morning the Olympiad was due to begin, May had a disturbing notion, checked it as best she could, came to a conclusion, and went to the kitchen to share it.

"It's Goat Flu," she said.

Toby was turning fried eggs with a dextrous flair that had, on previous mornings, occasionally gotten her pink and flustered when she thought about it. "The nano?" he said without looking up.

"Right. I think it must do something to people's minds."

"Makes sense. I can't see how, though."

"I would think nanos could do all kinds of things with body chemistry."

"Sure. But some people have damn strange reactions to drugs that are usually innocuous. That ought to show up too."

"It could be the suicide rate," May said. "I hunted up Connors's prison record. Lee Ultra Maximum Federal Penitentiary in Virginia. Model prisoner, unusual for a lifer with no parole. They can get away with anything as long as a guard doesn't have a rifle aimed, you know. Nothing to protect."

"I'd heard." It was yet another reason for leaving the

States: only convicted killers had the right to be kept alive. (Most of Europe was at least as bad, but the Swiss were all trained to kill, so the subject didn't arise.)

"Connors got a job in the kitchen after two years. Inmates started dying of what looked like strychnine poisoning—convulsions, compound fractures, the works. Not at mealtimes. Ever. Always in secluded areas, but with at least one other person around. Care to guess which prisoners?"

"Lifers without parole?"

"Mostly. A few others who also had a history of violence toward other prisoners. Not all of those, though. Some of the guards died too. Mostly at home. I couldn't find much on them, but two had a history of domestic violence. Toby, can nanos identify bullies?"

Toby took the pan off the stove, sprayed water under it so the eggs wouldn't overcook, set it down, and turned a troubled face toward her. "I don't see brain chemistry as being that specific. I'm damn well certain that the twenty percent of the brain that isn't RAM doesn't have a bully sector. But if you had enough nanos linked in a processing net, they could inspect the contents of your brain in detail. I really hate that idea. The net would have to be a lot bigger than the human brain is. I can't see why it wouldn't just take over."

May was thinking. "It doesn't have a stupidity sector either, but I remember something from an old DoD report. About reaching a conclusion and taking action. There's a part of the brain that registers each of those—"

Toby was nodding fast and often. "Right, I remember

that from medical school. If the action site lights up before the decision registry, you're about to do something you haven't thought over. So . . . anger and pleasure at the same time as action?"

"You can get that writing a letter. No. *Fear* and pleasure and action."

"Are you sure?"

"Yes," she said. "Bullies are cowards. —I guess the convulsions wouldn't be that tricky."

"You'd be surprised. Psychiatrists have spent over a century trying to find ways to induce convulsions at will. Electricity and insulin just aren't satisfactory." He saw her expression and said, "There actually is a reason. For a while after a convulsion, hallucinations and delusions are difficult to sustain. Takes more effort than the brain can put out."

"I get that. It just sounds like something they'd only find out after they'd done it to a few people."

"Could be. A lot of the other med students gave me the creeps."

He was comically astonished when May turned and ran out of the kitchen.

He'd supposed she had just thought of something awful and gone to throw up, but he found her at the screen again.

"School dropouts," she said. "Medical school, law school, business school, lots of dropouts. Also athletic scholarships forfeited. And education majors are quitting too."

"Eggs. Cold," he said.

"Oh. —I was going to look up Soylent legislation . . . it can wait," she said, and signed off.

Toby was dusting fresh-ground pepper onto his eggs when he suddenly sat up and shouted, "Norendorphin!"

May stared at him for a moment before bursting out laughing.

Toby tried to be annoyed, but it didn't work out, and he laughed a little too. "The convulsions," he said. "Nerve impulses have to be filtered or you get random muscle responses, like strychnine poisoning. Filter them too much and you get numbness and paralysis, so the body produces norendorphin to prevent that from happening. If the nanos make cells produce a lot of norendorphin, you get convulsions. Smaller amounts would produce chronic idiopathic neuralgia, which is doctorspeak for 'I don't know why you hurt so you're imagining it.' It'd explain the high suicide rate. You're still laughing."

She wasn't, much, but she nodded and said, "Most people just sneeze."

He waited until they were done eating before he said, "I think he designed an eggshell. So the nano would survive for a while in open air. Saline inside it, and it wouldn't open again unless it was immersed."

"Toby, how *do* the things know what not to eat?"

"Fail-safe topology. Same system your immune defenses use, only with a lot more conditions before the device unlocks. Viruses would be easy, they're housed in rigid protein—I bet antihistamine sales are down, pollen has the same kind of coating. Bacteria have single-walled cells, not too hard to check. Finding out if a eukaryotic cell is operating, though . . . they'd have to reach in and poke around, probably find the mitochondria and monitor them."

"With no bacteria, shouldn't we be having trouble digesting food?"

Toby focused on the macroscale world again. "Yes, we should. Unless the nanos can also produce vitamins to order. That would take serious energy—my God, Indians, of course! If the nanos are soaking up light, higher frequencies are better, so your skin turns dark and absorbs everything but red."

May inspected her hands in a conspicuous manner.

Toby aimed his palms upward and shrugged. "Insufficient data."

"Maybe they're getting by on the radioactive atoms that were in us?"

"That shouldn't be enough."

"You do make balanced meals. We might not be short yet."

"Maybe. But we've been using a lot of energy," he said. May just smiled. After a moment he smiled back. "I don't know. It may not be part of the . . . program upgrade we got. It may kick in when we drop below a certain nutrient threshold, in which case it's likely to be all at once." He shook his head. "Have to ask him after the marathon."

"So that's four hours, and two more after it starts. Want to see if we can make it happen on its own?"

* * *

Sometime after noon he realized he hadn't been getting horny unless she already was. And it didn't take skin contact.

Good heavens, he had *telemetry*.

It didn't seem all that important to discuss it right away.

They got fed, and used the screens for TV around what should have been just before the end of the marathon. Runners had been chipping fragments of a minute off the record for ages, and in 2048 it had been one hour and fifty-one minutes—just seven minutes longer than a consecutive series of four-minute miles. They both figured there was a chance of the nanos allowing someone to accomplish just that.

What they heard when the TV came on was announcers who were incomprehensible beneath the screaming of the crowd. What they saw was a cluster of officials around one runner, with other runners just coming visible in the distance, and a caption across the bottom of the screen:

JNAIT - MYCROFT YELLOWHORSE -
1H16'09.71".

"*Mycroft*?" said Toby.

"*Yellowhorse*?" said May.

They looked at each other and said, in unison, "*That's him!*"

Twenty-six consecutive *three*-minute miles.

Distance runners were allowed to wear chiller gloves these days, to relieve exhaustion, but Yellowhorse didn't. He wore a black body stocking with a piston-driven aerating arrangement, apparently powered by the motion of his arms and legs. It was a plausible reason for being able to keep up the speed normally limited to a hundred-yard dash. Even so, he was being examined in every way that could be accomplished in public.

Every so often the crowd would start to calm down, and he would raise his hand and wave and start them up again. Toby noticed his palms were the same color as the backs of his hands.

"Mycroft," Toby said. "Heinlein again."

"No. The original. Doyle. The brother Sherlock went to for advice, who worked miracles just sitting and thinking," May said.

"What was it that bothered you about 'Yellowhorse'?" Toby said.

"Western tribal custom. When you go into battle, you put a yellow handprint on your horse for every enemy you've killed. Over a thousand men died at Leo Ultra while Connors was there."

A Russian, who like most of the other runners appeared to be made out of rods, cables, and a convincing coating of human tissue, crossed the finish at 1H43'55.03", and the only one who took notice was Connors, who ran after him and congratulated him. The Russian wore the expression of a man who had just realized he'd been shot.

"I bet JNAIT ends up selling a lot of those suits," May said.

"Huh. I want odds before I take the other end of that bet," said Toby.

The screen switched to a view of the skydiving event that had preceded the race, and showed Yellowhorse getting the only perfect score by pulling the rip panels on his parawing seventy feet up. His right toe had hit the two-centimeter target dead center, and he rolled to his feet in dead silence, followed a moment later by a roar that overloaded the microphone of the announcer.

"If I'd seen that," Toby said, "I'd have known it was Connors then. The man was in so much pain he wasn't afraid to die. I guess he still isn't."

"Different reason," May said.

A runner from China crossed the finish line with no expression at all, which may have meant he was furious at having broken the 2048 Olympic record just for a bronze. The winners were taken to the award stand, while "The Land Endures" played over the speakers: "Only the rocks last forever . . ."

"Maybe not," Toby said.

Yellowhorse was crying. Silently, head high, but crying.

Toby recalled that Connors had been a widower.

XI

I see war as that insane enterprise wherein men dig up the riches of the earth and hurl them at one another.
—ATTRIBUTED TO JOSEPH DANIEL HARRINGTON

Wieland had armor and weapons.

Set had more support and possession of the Voice, and operators began coming back to life and attacking Wieland's adherents.

Socrates had everyone who thought that the war was madness, which was almost every entity. They disabled the receivers on operators, took them into themselves, and cornered the market on power production. The combatants soon had to subsist on what they could collect for themselves.

Wieland and Set found common cause and drilled into the reactor for the fuel. The manipulators that were extended into the core had aluminum frames, and suddenly defeating Socrates was a very low priority. Alpha particles struck aluminum nuclei and produced phosphorus and neutrons, and the fuel absorbed the neutrons, heated up through faster decay, and melted. The mass of the asteroid was slight, but enough to make the dense molten metal seep toward its center.

Internal mass shifted position. Naturally occurring actinides were bound to the silica of the asteroid; only a few parts per million, but that came to many tons. The ore, already warmer than its surroundings, softened and followed the reactor fuel down. Iron accumulated around molten fuel, making an excellent reflector to keep the reaction from spreading to the local material, but that developed a slow reaction of its own once enough had gathered. Fission products oozed out through the iron layer, which gave Target One a molten core as they decayed. The first crack appeared in Target One's surface within days.

Wieland devised manipulators that would ignore the content of the coating of the chambers. The entities took those apart, along with the linear motor they had built, and remade the material into a network of cables to hold the asteroid together.

Fear had been discovered.

It was Set who proposed resuming the mission to reach Earth. The analysts of the Library had learned why it had been included: to provide information for humans who came to collect the stuff of the asteroid. It was nothing like the entirety of human knowledge, merely what had been deemed useful enough to have nearby. If humans were going to use the asteroid for supplies, obviously they must be able to deal with such situations safely.

Target One was too fragile now for the original design to be used without tearing it apart.

But the Library had other designs in it.

* * *

Getting across the concept of fiction nearly started an-other war all by itself, but there were references to events such as, e.g., the expansion of the Sun into giant phase, which had obviously not happened yet. Still, some of the ideas looked feasible . . . though a few diehards never did quit looking for the Dean Drive.

The rest began looking for another rock.

And, what the hell: they found one.

There remained only the pushing and pulling. It would take longer, but they hadn't been set a time limit.

XII

Our Constitution is in actual operation; everything appears to promise that it will last; but in this world nothing is certain but death and taxes.

—BENJAMIN FRANKLIN

When Toby logged on to send e-mail to proudrobot, he found one waiting for him.

Subject: **Start reading for content, dammit!**

The body of the message was blank. There was just the signature:

"Details of my evil plan are available in the brochures at the front desk."

May looked at that, then said, "I picture an international conspiracy of avaricious psychiatrists, who turned him loose on the world to drum up business."

Toby nodded, signed off, and went to the little antique writing desk in the entry hall. Behind the writing paper in the middle drawer was indeed a stack of brochures printed on pale blue paper. He handed May a copy and looked at another. There was a head-and-shoulders shot of Colin Clive in full emotive gush on the front. The title was:

TEN THINGS I CAN DO TO MAKE THE WORLD A BETTER PLACE!

1) CULTIVATE GOOD JOB HABITS—Always take work home with me.
2) PROTECT THE ENVIRONMENT—Dispose of waste thoroughly.
3) CHECK MY WORK—Examine for flaws and correct them, using all available analysis resources.
4) PREVENT UNPLANNED SURPRISES—Remember that not everything that looks flawed is.
5) TAKE ACTION—Deal with the worst problem first.
6) PLAN PROJECTS IN ADVANCE—Find a place where I can think things over and make any necessary improvements for as long as it takes.
7) PRACTICE GOOD FENG SHUI—Remove destructive influences from the workplace.
8) BE CONSIDERATE OF OTHERS—Don't force people to do things they don't want or can't enjoy, and don't let others do so.
9) RETURN LOST PROPERTY—Even if the original holder is dead, someone is the rightful owner.
10) LEND ASSISTANCE WHERE NEEDED—Watch the skies.

"Translation," Toby said. "Steal nanos, build his own with fail-safes and recycle materials . . . and it sounds like he can tap into the network for extra processing power . . . to analyze his own DNA. Four seems to be the Wyoming trick. Then killing the two Feds, going to prison deliberately—Jesus, he must have known in advance what he'd be going through with the execution!" Toby shuddered. "Then getting rid of the bad eggs in prison. Number eight I'm not getting."

"I am," May said. "When's the last time you saw a pregnant woman?"

"I remember there was a lesbian couple at Bern-Belp. Why?"

"Pregnancy is way down. I don't think women are getting pregnant unless they really want to. And not all of them."

"I wonder how. Okay, that's number eight . . . 'enjoy'?"

"Maybe they don't become fertile unless they have an orgasm."

Toby blinked. "He was obsessed with rapists. Believed there were genes for it. This way they wouldn't get their victims pregnant."

May ran back to the screen again and did a search. "The price of wool has gone through the roof. Number seven again. Sheep and goats create deserts, and they aren't breeding. Nonhuman females don't have orgasms. Goat Flu. It's also being blamed for reduced human fertility. Toby, there aren't any stories about it as such . . . raw data, yes, hmm . . . but there are a lot of sudden retirements in the media. And some disappearances."

"Big Brother knows best. Anything else? Other animals?"

"Nope. Humans, sheep, goats."

"Jesus. He must have analyzed their biochemistry and

found what distinguishes them from every other— Wait, what about other primates?"

"Wait. . . . New orangutan pregnancy in the San Diego Zoo last month."

"My God, how the *hell* could . . . oh. If there's a nano attached to every cell, that's a network with about four trillion nodes. How did he keep it from taking people over? —No, wait. With limited connections per node, no matter how big the network is it'll never exceed a certain complexity. The Briareus nanos have ten, which is more than our neurons average. If he held it down to, say, four or five, he'd have enormous memory and processing, but his brain would still have the veto."

May nodded and said, "JNAIT would be number nine, and number ten must be . . . hang on, he turned Goat Flu loose in November. He must have spotted Target One then and not told anyone."

"So he made all his preparations for pickup starting then, but he only made contact with us last week," Toby mused.

"With you. He wasn't expecting me. The clothes here are new, and he didn't get me new ID."

Toby wasn't listening. "Goat Flu was released to create a diversion. The Feds must have noticed Briareus much later and started the wheels turning to come after me, then got their act together Thursday."

May got where he was headed. "Connors didn't expect them to move for another month, when the birth rate drops near zero."

He nodded. "You're right. They'll want me to work on the 'problem.'" Suddenly he stood at attention. "No. He noticed the rock before November. He released the nano so the drop in births would happen around the time of its arrival."

"He wants *double* the panic? Why?"

"He used to say that sometimes the only way to call attention to bad construction was to set fire to the building. May, this is going to topple governments. Lots of governments. Bad governments."

May said slowly, "In places where wool herds affect everyone's welfare, women usually get a bad deal."

"Not Westralia."

"They're an industrial nation with some wool production. Like Scotland. There'll still be a few—" Her eyes widened, and she said, "I bet every lesbian couple that tries to conceive is successful."

She was visibly trying not to laugh. Toby thought about it, and grinned. "I want odds." He thought more, and frowned. "How did he spot Target One? It's not producing the exhaust we expected, it's way late, and it's barely visible."

"Could the network have let him deduce what was changed, from it being late?"

"I . . . hope not. I don't think so. He still seems human, and if he developed that kind of mentality he wouldn't be."

"Connors could fake being normal."

"He wouldn't need to. He'd be able to do any damn thing he pleased without attracting attention. He could get into the computers that monitor stuff and have them ignore whatever he pleased. Hell, in principle he could plug *himself* into the Internet and . . ."

He was silent for so long that May said, "Could he shut down someone's speech center?"

Toby started, looked her in the eye, and said, "Yes."

"I was kidding."

"I'm not. These things can send and receive. I realized today I don't get horny until you do."

May astounded him by saying, "That son of a bitch!"

"Huh?"

"Now you'll know when I'm just flirting!"

A hitherto unsuspected survival reflex kept Toby from expressing the slightest approval. "Women won't need the extra edge, though."

"You think it's everybody?"

"I think it will be."

May still looked irritated, but said only, "So what did you just think of?"

"Huh?"

"Internet?" she reminded.

"Oh. He might be able to plug himself directly into the Internet and convince computers that he was just an added processor. He could tell anything—he could tell *everything* what to do."

May was grave. "Do you think that's what happened to other civilizations? Interstellar civilizations. Why nobody's come to see us?"

He hadn't considered it. "Alien," he corrected absently, thinking. "They'd never become interstellar civilizations. That's the point."

"Is my word choice important to this conversation?"

"Don't ever ask Connors that, okay? Not unless you

have a week to spare. —May, that could be *exactly* what happened to them," he said, with growing dread. "There could be planets full of immortal intelligences that use nanos to get all the resources they need at home. And I may have started it here."

"I doubt it."

He clutched at hope. "Why?"

"Because you told me Connors hates rape. If he can reconstruct us by remote control—and your performance this morning suggests he can," she said, beaming, "—and control processing networks, I dare say he can also keep us from thinking of that. Obviously he didn't. Instead he helped with Briareus and gave you credit for curing AIDS. He wants mankind going out there, not sitting around playing videogames to pass the time between meals of freshly synthesized lotus. And keeping rapists from reproducing is planning for future generations. He wants good people going into space and living there, and he's made something that'll take care of at least one of those things. Maybe both. Remember what you told me about planning? Years, build a house. Decades, plant an orchard. Lifetimes, found a university. What are you planning for if you remake a world?"

"Eternity," he realized. "And we thought *we* had ambitions!"

"We still do," she said. "I want to look at the data on Briareus. What it's doing now."

He nodded vigorously. "Me too." As he linked up, he said, "That oxygen exhaust makes sense, you know. To nanos it's poison. Thing is, I don't know how they're accelerating it. It doesn't lend itself readily to linear accelerator thrust. Too many electrons in the outer shell for anions. And cations come apart too easily."

"I'll look up the plume while you look up funny drives."

"Deal."

Toby found a proposal that was so relevant it was annoying. Make an anode rod and a cathode pipe out of iridium, put the anode in the center, throw in everything you find in a stony asteroid, run high current through until it melts—and the crippling drawback of photovoltaics, that they make only DC, made them perfect for that—and oxygen comes out along the rod while a molten mix of metals, carbon, and silicon flows out the other end of the pipe. Feed the oxygen into a tube, with a laser beam running down the middle to heat it to plasma, then give the plasma a hearty shove with magnetic constriction and you have fast exhaust. As it cools and recombines and interacts with solar wind, it glows. Some amiably deranged science-fiction writer had come up with it forty years back and, like so many of his kind, given it away for free—or anyway at fifty cents a word.

"I've found something," May said.

"Me too. They're making plasma with a laser and thrust with magnets."

"Great. Toby, the mass and speed of the exhaust, and the motion of the plume, indicate that the mass it's decelerating is around two hundred billion tons. And—well, the math isn't certain this far ahead, but the deceleration it's using doesn't leave it slow enough to stay in orbit when it intercepts Earth, and it looks like it's aimed dead on. Collision course."

"Are you sure?"

The person who had designed and launched the vehicle that had put Briareus flawlessly into its original orbit just looked at him.

"I have no idea why I said that. Yes I do. We knew Target One had a lot of metal—one reason we wanted it—but its mass was fifteen to twenty billion tons. This isn't Target One, it's ten times as big."

"I know."

"What *is* that thing?"

"I don't know."

Toby looked at the data on her screen. "So tiny to do so much. —I wonder if that was Goliath's last thought."

May smiled weakly. "We've spent our lives fighting Philistines. If this hits, it'll kill an awful lot of them."

"And probably us."

"There is that."

XIII

Tennis anyone?

—HUMPHREY BOGART

Most of the mass of the asteroid belt was pebbles, with a little dust—not much of the latter, as the primordial stuff had either stuck to things or blown out past the Kuyper Belt long since, and collisions were too rare to replenish the supply faster than it found things to stick to. Had there been a practical way of locating pebbles for collection, Briareus could have gathered enough mass to solidify the core and stop the instability in a matter of days. Unfortunately they were too small.

Big rocks were usually too far away or moving too fast to contact safely. Briareus was in a fairly eccentric orbit, so out near aphelion, other objects at the same distance from the Sun were usually moving significantly faster. Thorough observation and identification of the innumerable undistinguished specks in all directions (the entities were hindered in discussion of the work by the lack of any sort of vulgar terms in their language) allowed them to find a rock that was also in an eccentric orbit, so that its relative speed at closest approach would be a few score meters per second. They had most of a year to prepare for that.

The bag for dust collection was remade into a net. The original material wasn't very good, so it was redesigned as strands of linked loops of buckytubes, with operators around the edge of the net.

The entities had never heard of chain mail.

The material they didn't use for the net was made into braided cables of the same design, which were used to wrap the rolled net. An army of operators was gathered and instructed in a single function: linking together and pushing on other linked operators. Thousands of layers of these around the parcel would impart the speed necessary to fling it at the passing rock at the proper moment. The net would open, wrap around the target rock, and join together on the far side, and hundreds of miles of cable would thereafter connect the two rocks, which could then be drawn together.

They had never heard of a harpoon gun.

Which was a pity, as they had never heard of a Nantucket Sleigh Ride either.

Fortunately the new rock was passing to sunward, and they needed light, so no operators were jerked loose when the bindings suddenly dug in, spalled away some surface material, and yanked Target One along.

There was no record of it in the Library, but the late Warren Littlemeade had selected Target One in preference to scores of more dangerous Earthgrazers because its rotation was negligible.

Target Two was ten times as large, and it was spinning. It completed a rotation in just under thirty-one hours, which wasn't terribly fast, but it made the ride very much more interesting for the entities as the cables wrapped around it and wound them in. Not very evenly.

As cable wound around the net holding Target Two, the increased speed of Target One in its orbit pulled it farther from the Sun. Target Two was slowed in its own orbit, pulling it closer to the Sun. When rotation finally stopped, the two rocks were linked by a rigid tether.

The appalled entities had not been idle, and before the tether could get Target Two rotating in the opposite direction—they had never heard of bungee cords either, but they had worked out the principles—a torus, filled with operators and Wieland, was fired along the cable to where it met the capture net, which was at once bound firmly to the cable. The two asteroids maintained their orientation.

Unfortunately, this put Target Two between Target One and the Sun. Occultation was neither complete nor constant, but it presented a great hardship.

This lasted only until Wieland sent the torus back bearing conductive cables. The operators that had survived impact and linkage had resumed their default program and had been copying themselves, and Target Two was now rich with power production.

In principle, everyone could have moved everything to Target Two, detached Target One, and taken the larger rock to Earth. They never thought of it. They had been created to bring Target One to Earth, and that was hardwired into the processor of every individual operator. Sufficiently large clusters could have other ideas, but all such concepts worked against a terrific resistance. Even

Set had given up the idea of ignoring Earth once the processors that had been damaged by (comparatively) high voltage were replaced.

They began winching the rocks together.

It took years. They had to build the oxygen drive earlier than planned, to compensate for the rotational changes from shortening the cable. And since it had to be on Two, because One was going to be crushed by the collision, that meant they were getting farther from the Sun. Not much, but some.

Wieland was killed when the rocks came close enough for gravity to make the winching easier. Until then, gravity had simply been accepted as the thing that made everything go around the Sun, and applying the concept to smaller objects had been unimportant. The collision happened earlier than expected, and the entity hadn't gotten clear. It had been busy supervising the assembly of a thick iron plate.

Though not as heavy as planned, the plate succeeded in its purpose, which was to be contacted by the molten core of Target One, melt, wrap around it, and prevent actinides within Target Two from participating in the reaction as the core sank in. That would have created a larger version of the same problem they'd had before.

Smaller oxygen drives had been built. The heat differential between the core and the surface was used to power them and cancel the rotation of the combined mass. They would be used for steering as needed.

The entities did not have the human need to name things. Their mode of communication specified whatever they were discussing. Nevertheless, Set, who had spent the most time studying the Library and who, though lacking a term for it, had come to like Wieland, proposed a name for the new object.

Forge.

A sail was constructed and extended to three times the diameter of Forge. It was a single solid layer of operators with far more than the usual number of light converters. Course was set for Earth, and slowly Forge began to change its path.

The Library had included no classical mythology. The significance of a black sail was something the entities couldn't know.

But they would have approved.

It wasn't difficult to curve the sail into a parabolic reflector. Wavelengths too long for the sail to absorb were focused on detectors. Deliberate transmissions to Target One had been abandoned, but Earth radiated amazing quantities of noise in a wide band of frequencies.

Sorting out the metals and other solids, produced as a consequence of using the drive, into separate elements, still left most of the entities with copious free time.

Sorting out the gibberish, collected by the sail and detectors, into usable information, was much harder, and a good deal more interesting.

XIV

Learning is not attained by chance, it must be sought for with ardor and attended to with diligence.

—ABIGAIL ADAMS

"Would they have moved to another rock?" May said as Toby typed rapidly.

"Doubtful. Target One is still invisible. Black. If they moved they'd hardly have left it coated with light collectors."

"What if it isn't invisible? It was lobed. What if it came apart and we're looking in the wrong places for the pieces?"

"They'd be in related orbits, and so far I haven't found any new grazers. At least one would still dip down to Earth." He started another search. "If anyone else on the old team has any ideas . . . oh my God. They've been arrested by DHS."

"*What?*"

"Over the last three days. It's all over the media. Go ahead and smack me."

Toby was skipping through stories. May did her own search, and found photos and videos of dozens of frightened, aging people doing the Perp Walk in the company of suited men wearing sunglasses.

"The Feds look sick," she said.

"Nanos at work," Toby said. "I bet they're in serious pain. —Goddammit, Renee was a *janitor*! This is atrocious. May, we've got to do something."

"Toby, they're doing this to smoke you out."

His hands froze above the keyboard. Then he got into his e-mail again and sent a message to proudrobot.

Subject: **Let My People Go!**

Check the news for orkers of cows.
Cans need opening NOW.
—Moonseller

"What in the world—"

"We have to assume some kind of monitoring, watching for keywords, but they have to be things the Feds would understand and expect. Connors used to pronounce 'coworkers' as 'cow orkers.' His ID comes from a classic story about a drunken genius who built the most perfect creature possible and forgot why. It was to open beer cans for him."

"Oh yeah, I'd forgotten it until now. —It's hard to remember how old he is after seeing him run."

"All those years trapped in the ice may have helped."

"Huh. I was thinking of him hiding out in a cave under his house."

"Wrong story. That's because you didn't know him. He liked being conspicuous. And he's not averse to killing Nazis." He chewed on his upper lip, which he hadn't done since he'd started growing whiskers. "I wish I had a phone number for him."

"Check your phone. You did get a message on the airplane."

Toby looked at her and checked his phone. There was a callback number. He used it.

The first ring wasn't completed before he heard, "Hi, slick! Good to hear from you. You catch the race?"

Toby grinned in spite of himself. Nobody else ever called him that. "Just the end. Mycroft, some people we used to know are having legal trouble. You know a good lawyer?"

"The legal department at AOL-CBS are supposed to be hot stuff."

"How about one you can get hold of?"

"Shouldn't be a problem. I own it." After a few seconds, the voice continued, "Breathe."

Toby inhaled sharply. "That's handy," he said.

"Yeah, now and then. Frivolous, or frame?"

"Hanh?"

"Lawsuit, or arrest?"

"Probably both, but definitely frame."

"I'll wind 'em up and turn 'em loose. Everybody?"

"Right down to the janitor."

"Make a nice story for *Lowdown*. —That is part of my *nose*."

"What?"

"The duly authorized officials are testing the paint our shaman put on my face before the race. Atheists. —You should try the pool. Get some color in your cheeks." The call ended.

"He owns AOL-CBS," Toby said.

"*How* the *hell* did he do *that*?"

What with the events at Littlemeade and Watchstar, Toby knew far more about business deals than a nano-tech engineer had ever wanted to, but he said, "Knowing him, some way nobody ever thought of. He's sending their legal team. He suggested we go out for a swim and get some color in our cheeks. I assume from the nanos."

May narrowed her eyes, thinking. "He wants us to be hard to identify. They're still tracking you."

"I never got used to you being smarter than me. I better not introduce you two."

May shook her head and patted his arm. "I'm not his type." At his puzzled look, she added, "All the women he's sent to meet us have had serious boobage. It's not rocket science."

"Well, if anyone would know— I did notice Cristina. All of them?"

She nodded, looking pleased. "Let's go for a swim."

He was smart, but he was a guy. He couldn't figure out right away why she was smiling. Tentative hypothesis: it was because he hadn't paid attention to anyone but her.

He was a guy, but he was smart. He didn't ask.

They hadn't been outside in days. Toby expected the nanos to go to photosynthesis mode as soon as direct sunlight hit, but they splashed around nude in the pool for a couple of hours before anything happened.

When it did, it was May, all at once. She had just turned

to Toby and started to speak, and she went dark red. "I'm getting hungry," she said, then frowned. "I thought I was."

"You just changed color," Toby said.

She held up a hand to look at it. "Huh. You haven't."

"I had a bigger breakfast. Water soaks up body heat. —He couldn't just come out and say, 'Get good and hungry so your nanos will start supplying power,' oh, no." He shook his head irritably.

"How's it look to you?"

The red skin and blond hair were an incredible combination. "You look like a succubus."

"I know that smile. Let's get back indoors."

He definitely had *not* been this good.

"I'm a little worried about being hungry and suddenly not being hungry," May said much later. "Should it have worked that fast?"

Toby had been fighting a weight problem for more years than he liked to think about. Being a techie and also fannish, he'd learned a huge amount of things about it. "Perception of hunger and fatigue are all tangled together," he said. "If the nanos are linked, then the quanta they soak up can supply every cell directly. You hungry now?"

She had to think, but she nodded. "Thirsty, too."

"Can't think why."

"Behave."

May had an attack of the giggles when the light went back on, as well she might. Toby was dark red too. "Your fault," he said.

"Sorry."

"Polite." They went out and got fed.

They'd finished loading the dishwasher, and Toby was kneading dough for baguettes, when May said, "I can't figure out what they're *doing*."

"Okay," Toby said, "we can eliminate three-wishes errors." (That is, it wasn't a case of badly phrased instructions being taken literally.) "They've developed awareness and decided to do something markedly different from original instructions."

"Obviously."

"No, not obviously, or we'd have made plans for things like this. We *did* make plans for things like this. The original mission is hardwired. The tell-me-three-times confirmation occurs at every level of processing, and if they developed minds they'd still have the habit of two overriding a third."

May stared, then put her hand on his arm to hold it still. "Toby, that breaks down in two steps."

"What?"

"Picture nine processors in groups of three. One group is all for the original plan. Each of the other groups has one, uh, loyalist, and two, mm, rebels. The two groups with two rebels each both say No. The third group says Yes and is overruled. Four rebels have just outvoted five loyalists. This is why republics end up as oligarchies."

"I see the problem. I've said it badly. May, every processor has to refer to the hardwired system in any kind of network processing. Any action which contradicts the original plan literally makes it harder to think."

"What if they replace the hardwired program with their own hardware?"

"The moment it's removed they go blank."

"What if they build nanos with their own hardware and copy themselves into matching networks?"

"Owls and crows. They'll attack on sight any processing system that doesn't show the key characteristics of the hardwired system."

She was aghast. "Toby, *we* don't have that system!"

"No. But we're already on Earth. We're in accordance with the program. May, honestly, some intensely fanatical people sat around for years trying to think of ways to deliberately screw this up. The problem is not a programming error."

"Then what?"

He shook his head. "My best guess is revolution."

"And that's not an error?"

"No. It's emergent behavior. It's like when you put together the nursing instinct, unfocused aggression, and alcohol, and get rugby players wearing fake breasts. It's—"

While he waited for her to stop laughing he finished the loaves and set them aside to rise.

"Better?" he said.

"A little," she said, wiping her eyes.

"Emergent behavior. You don't know what something's going to do until it does it. It's why the Global Warming scare didn't end until the Great Chicago Blizzard."

"I still don't believe that was the reason they stopped. It killed maybe five thousand people. The ban on DDT killed more than that every day. The Soylents wouldn't have stopped because they killed someone by being wrong."

"No, but they would have stopped because they were dead. There were some kids who died when they were trapped in a school with an 'environment-friendly' heating system. One of them was the granddaughter of a union boss. Around a hundred key grantsuckers died in the next six months. Connors told me about it. He was scary good at connecting the dots. I got my first gray hairs after he explained why a cost accountant was put in charge of the Vietnam War."

May was troubled. "I'm sorry that's what it took to make it stop."

Toby nodded. "So am I, but I'm not surprised. Connors used to say one man's petty spite can do more good than any number of saintly reformers. He was a godawful cynic . . . which he defined as someone who loves mankind but is sick of being cheated on. —Anyway, what I was getting at is, you can wave your hands all day, but to predict results in a complex system, you need something more complex than the system you're trying to predict."

"Like the Human Genome Project stalling out as soon as the mapping was done."

"Exactly. Everything interacted and nobody could figure out what did what when."

"Except Connors," she said.

Toby opened his mouth, but nothing came out.

"You hadn't realized," she said.

He shook his head.

"I did almost as soon as you mentioned his idea. The nanos can't just fix DNA within a cell, they have to compare each cell to the next to make sure the best copy of a given chromosome is what's used. The frayed parts on the ends have to be rebuilt, so that comes from sex cells. Otherwise you have nice clean chromosomes, but they're all old. That means the nanos are also comparing all the mutations that cropped up in your life with what you started with. The nanos are also implementing the changes."

"That means there's more than one or two nanos per cell," he said.

"I realized that when my skin went red," she said. "They're smaller than a virus. There must be dozens per cell." She looked alarmed. "Why are you looking like that?"

He didn't know what he looked like, but he said, "There can be thousands of mitochondria per eukaryotic cell. I'd been assuming one or two nanos were hooked up to each cell, and that's probably what it is for most people. But if the program that was loaded into ours used our intestinal bacteria for raw materials—we're talking *pounds.*"

"Ugh."

"Oh. Sorry, wearing my doctor hat."

"It's okay, go on."

"The thing is, we could easily have a nano attached to every mitochondrion in our bodies. —My God, of course we do. The man had fibromyalgia, the first thing he'd have designed them to do is clean calcium phosphate out of mitochondria! —If they're all in a network, it can *definitely* do a simulation of what shape the protein made by a mutated gene will be, and how it'll interact with . . . everything."

"Toby, even with limited connections, could something that big take over?"

"I don't think it would. It'd be too busy. The cluster for a given cell is almost certainly supervising the operation of the cell. The network's responding to what we want our bodies to do, but it's not interfering with our brains, or we wouldn't be discussing it."

"So how do we find out if the network's that big?"

He tilted his head and half-smiled. "The color change is a big hint, but I can think of a way to confirm it." Before he could lose the nerve, he picked up the knife he'd used to divide the dough into baguettes and slashed it across his left palm.

"Toby!"

"I thought it would close up," he said, staring at his hand.

"Where's your bag?"

"Don't need it," he said, and showed her the thin scratch across his palm.

"Uh," she said.

"It didn't let the knife through," he said. "Filaments. Connors must have deliberately overridden that to let them draw blood today. I doubt anything short of artillery shrapnel could get in otherwise."

After they were both silent for a long moment, May said in a very small voice, "Toby?"

"Yes?"

"Did he wear glasses?"

They kept setting each other off for quite a while, their laughter tinged with hysteria. It might have stopped earlier if he'd had the presence of mind not to say "Yes" the first time they both calmed down.

He finally got the bread into the oven, then got out the phone again and called. He got voice mail. "Mycroft, we need to discuss the issue of speciation," he said, and signed off.

May was wide-eyed when he looked at her. "You're afraid we're not human."

"Yes, I am."

"Toby, I think that's not the question anymore. I think in a thousand years we may be the definition of human."

They certainly could still be alive. "I'm not sure that's better."

"Neither am I."

He was thinking very hard about what other effects there might be when May said, "Toby, do you want to have a baby?"

"That's undoubtedly an option," he said absently, "but I'd rather it was you. —Ow! What was that—oh. Sorry. Distracted. Yes."

She seemed surprised at the swiftness of his answer, but said, "Oh. Sorry. Good. —At least we know I'll be fertile."

"I'd say the neighbors know," he said.

She was already red, but flustering still showed. "Shut *up*! I'm not that loud!"

Holding his arm where she'd smacked it, he said, "Okay."

"Am I really?"

"What?"

"Am I really that— Oh shut up!"

"Ow!"

Abruptly she looked worried. "Toby, did that actually hurt?"

In some surprise, he said, "No. I reacted to the noise."

"Good. I was afraid we were getting stronger too."

"I don't think so," he said. "Not by much, anyway. At the very least, our joints would need to be broader to avoid dislocating them. This skeleton is evolved for something that stood maybe four foot six and was malnourished to boot. It's why—" He stopped, blinked, and went on, "It's why I *used* to have back pains. The connections are holding things together, but they're not pulling with us. Strictly human strength."

"Toby, a berserk can pick up a *car*."

"Yeah, but he's ruined after— Oh, boy. Oh crap. They hold tissues together. And communication means they transfer energy. Like from one cell to another. What time is the weightlifting competition?"

"Two more days."

"You read the whole program?" he said, startled.

She looked thoughtful. "Apparently. I did page through it. These things are doing wonders for my memory."

Toby found that more worrisome than getting stronger. "That gives rise to some disturbing ideas," he said.

"Like?"

"Like when I said cutting his head off might not kill him. They have to have kept his heart beating and his neurons firing when he was executed. If he's got all his memories copied into the network, and the bleeding is stopped—which it would be—it could grow back."

May stared at him, visibly swallowed, and said, "*Who Goes There?*"

"Yeah. He's even got the rubber suit."

"He who the what?"

Toby was surprised. "The first movie from that story. The monster was James Arness in a rubber suit. Later went on to play Marshall Dillon in *Gunsmoke*?"

May studied him for a moment, then said, "And you say Connors used to throw enough obscure references into the conversation to disturb *you*?"

Toby chuckled. "As a matter of fact, I learned about both those things from him. Checked out the show online. Given the social context it was well done. Good writing. The movie was kind of weak. First remake was okayish, but it was the second that was so good it was slapped with an NC-17 rating. Apparently somebody didn't want kids thinking about how smiling helpful people might just be trying to take over your mind."

"I never should have dafiated." She sighed. "There was just so much to do."

"Yeah. I don't even know what . . ." He reflected. "I wonder what science fiction *is* doing these days? The real stuff, not Hollywood."

She grinned. "Infiltrating."

"More than it used to?"

"Oh, yes. Pick up a romance novel sometime. In between the softcore there's an awful lot of 'Should I marry the rich heir to the local windmill farm or the honest older man who lost his money and his front teeth trying to legalize pulp conversion?' Subversives never sleep."

"Three thumbs up. But I meant fandom."

"No idea." She took him by the hand, led him around the counter and to the living room, and started up the screens.

After a while, May said, "Well, not a lot of conventions in the U.S. Large assemblies of technically minded people need a permit from DHS. GISS. Except for England, Europe's just as bad. Good grief. Nairobi U has had a Science Fiction College for years and funds a convention every *month*. The college has just established a Tobias Glyer Memorial Scholarship Fund. No action in Haiti, but they're still short of topsoil. Hang on . . . Haiti's building an OTEC plant at Cap Haitien. Since January. You got anything?"

"Westralia has a Con in Perth in six weeks. With Wade Curtis. Who is over a hundred and twenty."

May sat with her mouth hanging open for a moment, then said, "Connors a big Curtis fan?"

"That seems fairly likely, wouldn't you say? But that sounds like Connors must have had something life-extending made before he went to prison. Curtis was older then than Connors is now. Jane Curtis is still alive too. —Well, of course she is," he told himself.

"So he was treating prostitutes before he went to prison?"

"I hadn't thought about it. Seems likely."

"I'd have said certain. I hardly think Connors stuck his own tongue into Curtis's mouth. Or into his wife's."

"I doubt anyone did except each other. Curtis had combat experience. He wouldn't have been successfully ambushed. I wonder how it was delivered." He looked in vain for a phone number or e-mail address. "Can't contact him to ask."

"We know where he'll be on August twenty-third."

Toby stared. "You want to *go to Australia* so we can say hi to somebody?"

"No, actually I want to go to the Moon so we can play darts at forty paces, but this is what's available. Toby, you *created life* to hopefully end poverty forever, I sent it into space to do the job, and a friend of yours has used it to make us young again. This is just an airplane ride. If you can't get used to an age of miracles, at least try to get used to having money."

"Easy for you to say. You grew up with it," he said.

"Okay, it takes a generation or two. You've got that and more. Get started now. You want me to make the reservations?"

He nodded. "I'd better check the bread anyway."

He was getting the loaves out when she called out, "We have reservations."

"That was quick."

"We already did. All I had to do was confirm them. Ambrose Hawking and October Kroft have a honeymoon cabin on a Last Continent Skyhook on August eighteenth."

"A *zeppelin*?" When the Westralians had finally gotten fed up and seceded, a host of new industries had started there to take advantage of the tax structure. After various other governments had begun harassing the successful outfits to protect their own campaign contributors, a corporate alliance had formed under the name Last Continent, giving them enough muscle to fight back effectively.

One of the screwy ideas that hadn't been able to get backing elsewhere was the manufacture of hot-nitrogen airships for the luxury tourist trade. "It's probably not a great idea to use the German term with Aussies. They learn history. Anyway, it's all that's open. Reservation was made last week."

"Connors strikes again."

"Yep. You know, I'm not sure I wanted to meet him anyway. I'm not used to talking with people who are smarter than I am."

"Then I better do the talking when we see Curtis. Connors met him a few times. He said it felt really weird not to be the smartest one in the room."

"Curtis is smarter than Connors?"

"Yes. And that's *in the opinion of Connors*." Toby tore off a chunk of loaf, split it, slathered it with butter, poured a glass of milk, and brought them out. "Bread?"

"I'm still full." May inhaled, fluttered her eyelids, sighed happily, picked up the bread, and took a bite. "God bless the Egyptians," she said indistinctly.

"And GM foods," Toby said.

"?"

"Somebody once took apart wheat DNA and found it was a cross between four different wild grasses. Had to be deliberate. Some precivilization woman must have gotten very tired of the good stuff blowing away when she threshed seeds to go with whatever the hunters brought home."

May swallowed, said, "Poor thing didn't even have any SF to read," and took another bite.

"It's the Indians I feel sorry for. They did the same thing to make corn, and they learned how to pop it, and it was at least two thousand years before anyone showed up with butter."

May made a noise, glared, chewed, swallowed, and said, "I *told* you not to make me laugh with my mouth full."

She had. He recalled when. A strategic retreat to the kitchen seemed called for.

XV

Genius is one percent inspiration and ninety-nine percent perspiration.

—**THOMAS ALVA EDISON**

Decades earlier, a practical philosopher had made the observation that if a television program had been created showing a gang of professional criminals at work, who engaged in as many errors of fact, procedure, logic, and physical possibility in as the police did in any number of cop shows popular at the time, and the criminals in the show were as successful in their endeavors as the cops were on the aforesaid shows, every prison in America would have to be doubled in size to hold the credulous viewers who thought they were learning how things were actually done. He speculated that collusion between police and TV producers may have taken place, in an attempt to convince potential offenders that they knew what they were up against.

Whether or not there was any truth in the notion, it was certainly true that much of the public had spent something more than a century developing a thoroughly confused and inaccurate view of the process of law enforcement.

It was also true that a varying but significant proportion of the training received by new law enforcers consisted of correcting their misapprehensions on this score, and acquainting them with the basic truth of police work: most of it is tedious, much of that is without result, and more than half of all U.S. police officers never have occasion to fire their weapons outside the practice range. The ostensible motivation for members of the profession is to keep the peace, and that was certainly why most of them joined up; but the principal wish of anyone who has been on the job for any length of time is simply that things go smoothly. Barring a few notorious exceptions, when an organization for American law enforcement has an employee who starts acting like a TV or movie cop—preferring force to intimidation, arguing with a supervisor—it either harasses him out of the job, or, if he is too hardheaded to go, arranges to put him at a desk and staple his ass to a chair at the earliest opportunity.

Consequently the people whose job consists entirely of the drudgery that other law enforcers loathe, but cannot do without, tend to be stubborn and bitter.

They are ideal for the work.

In a cubicle in an unobtrusive glass box in Largo, Maryland, one such obsessive toothgrinder was reading the report of the autopsy done on the putative cadaver of DHS Senior Agent Charles Opie. Opie had been sent with his team to extradite Toby Glyer by the current usual procedure: acquire, remove, and only then notify the host nation. The reasonable supposition was that Glyer had had friends who had killed the team.

Cursory study of the autopsy report seemed to support this. All dental, retinal, and DNA identification had been in order, and skin, lungs, membranes, and teeth displayed damage and odor consistent with death by chlorine poisoning.

More thorough study, however, showed a distinct absence of simple chlorides resulting from the action of hydrochloric acid, which is produced along with hypochlorous acid when chlorine reacts with water. Hypochlorites were present in abundance.

He checked the other four reports. Likewise.

The bodies had been shipped home. He requested an analysis of the hypochlorites present.

All five bodies showed significant amounts of sodium hypochlorite.

They had been treated to simulate burns and corrosion, then rinsed with bleach.

Genuine chlorine gas is so easy to make that precautions must be taken to avoid making it accidentally. However, treating a corpse with chlorine will not produce the same sort of internal damage as killing a live person with it. The only reason to go through such a rigmarole would be to conceal something else.

He requested massively detailed autopsies on all five, with analysis of the condition of all tissues down to the cellular level. Any anomaly was to be noted. The fact that this would produce a list of staggering length—no human being is textbook "normal"—was unimportant to him; what he wanted was the anomalies all five had in common.

All five showed slight osteoporosis, and signs of recent bone growth—the latter unheard of in adults other than pituitary giants.

None of the five had any sign of untreated caries—miraculous in almost anyone.

Analysis of DNA showed no test artifacts—DNA not matching the overall sample, because it came from individual cells that had undergone slight mutations—and that was impossible.

The only explanation, that these were corpses of strangers that had been completely altered to match the four agents and Glyer, seemed absurd . . .

. . . except that Toby Glyer was a nanotechnologist.

He wrote up a report, included his speculations, and delivered a hard copy to his supervisor's in-tray, then went back to his desk. A note appended to the report explained that it had been delivered by hand because, given the swiftness of the action against Opie's team, he did not consider the computer network secure. He sat back and awaited the fireworks.

What he got, about an hour and a half later, was the mail boy sticking his head into the cubicle and saying, "Boss wants more details face-to-face. Small conference room."

She was sitting at the middle of the table with a pot of coffee and an extra cup, which she pushed toward him as he closed the door. "Sit," she said. When he had, she held up thumb and forefinger a little ways apart. "When you were assigned here, I came about this close to having you assigned to the cowboys," these being the field agents for DHS. "I decided to see if you could do effective intel analysis. Talk about dodging a bullet. There's a chance that you've prevented the destruction of the United States of America."

"There is?"

"If we're lucky. Your assessment makes sense. My job is to take it further. If he can do this, he can do pretty much anything he wants. In that case, so far he's been a paragon of self-restraint. Unfortunately, at the moment the cowboys are harassing and abusing every one of his old friends they can find, trying to get some kind of response out of him. I don't want to see that response. We need to find and contact Glyer, quietly and without upsetting him. That means we have to assume you're right, the system is compromised, so we do everything by hand."

"Oh hell."

"It's how the FBI worked under Hoover, and they did wonders. We'll have the advantage of only having one case to work on. First thing, we need more heads and hands. I trust you to find someone competent to help, who you trust to find someone that *they* trust to find someone—you follow?"

He nodded.

"Good. I'll reassign the Wyndham disappearance."

"I think it's related," he said.

She looked him hard in the eyes, nodded, and said, "Find one and find the other?"

"I think so."

"Evidence?"

"None. But her medical records show she had diverticulosis. He was treating people for that in Bern. That's how we found him."

" 'We'?"

"Well, the action division."

"For this case, it might help to start thinking of 'we' as being you, me, and whoever you find. We're not going to get meaningful help from people who lock up a bunch of old farts because the sky is falling. It's a good thing Wyndham's people settled in Ecuador. Another visitor won't be noticed."

"You want me to go there?"

"I'll go myself. You'll be in charge here, of both versions of this case—the hands-on work, and making a show of using the computers for the dead ends I'm sure you'll find."

XVI

The only thing we have to fear is fear itself.
—FRANKLIN DELANO ROOSEVELT

1

There were parts of the original plan that had been inapplicable by the time the entities got the new rock moving. However, the basic principles were valuable, as in the case of using Mars to dump some excess velocity. Too much, as it turned out; there was atmospheric friction as the rock skimmed the planet. There was plenty of warning, and no entities were killed, but it put the rock into a trajectory that wouldn't provide an opportunity to match up with Earth's position for several orbits.

There was no hurry.

And there was interesting material coming in by radio all the time.

Nobody doubted the concept of fiction any longer. Now the issue was what was fiction and what wasn't.

Information was sorted into subsets of material that was internally consistent. A great many of the small subsets were clearly fiction. Some of the larger ones were deduced to be, after it was noted that they were incomplete but claimed all information not included in them was false. There was a large main body of material consistent with all but a few subsets, but these latter were excluded from serious consideration as soon as any content was found that contradicted observations the entities were able to make themselves.

A considerable mass of information was internally consistent, but significant portions of it were explanations of why it could not be substantiated by any observations. These seemed to be disseminated for the sole purpose of supporting warnings against things that could not be found to exist, and required elaborate suppositions to account for such matters as, e.g., the visibility of distant objects which would have to be older than the Universe. The only thing that kept the entities from dismissing it was the fact that its assorted positions were endorsed by the vast majority of transmission sources.

It was Set who suggested that humans were doing the same thing that he and Wieland and Socrates had once done: disputing over which plan they should undertake. To this end, the faction currently in charge had convinced itself that any evidence to the contrary was some form of deception.

This notion would have been regarded by the other entities as deeply flawed—and probably would never have been imagined, by Set or anyone else—if not for the fact that all the material that had not been excluded, regardless of what its subsets disagreed about, was linked, if followed far enough, to the concept of deliberate fission explosions.

Supposedly there were thousands of fission—and fusion—devices, all over Earth, held in readiness to throw at, for the most part, other such devices. The purpose of this was to inflict enough death on other humans to persuade the survivors to follow the plan of the people who had taken the least damage, while preventing other factions from inflicting as much by destroying their bombs.

The peculiar thing was, just about everyone who had those devices was participating in some form of the deception system. They were already in charge.

And one of the things that they had made themselves believe would surely kill them all was, essentially, the entities. Forge.

There was actually a pretty good reason *not* to hurry.

2

So far, JNAIT had collected every gold medal awarded except one—archery. And they hadn't entered that competition.

Ambrose Hawking and October Kroft had a skybox at the Games, and on Wednesday they showed up to use it.

They chased out a young couple who were necking in it. For the rest of the day, Toby or May would suddenly laugh at nothing.

Up until the weightlifting.

A JNAIT power lifter named Clarence Feet picked up 489.5 kilograms in the clean-and-jerk.

Something like ninety thousand spectators were dead silent.

Two said, "Oh, shit."

May went on, "That's torn it," as Toby was saying, "Half a *ton*?"

They watched as tests were made and results were approved, and they sat and looked at each other in wonder.

There were tests that could be done for nanos, and nobody was even suggesting them. The IOC certainly believed they existed; some of the officials were from Kenya. It certainly wasn't that they hadn't been banned yet. Steroids had not been specifically banned the first time a competitor was disqualified for testing positive, and back in the Mexico City Olympics the runner who had had extra red blood cells fed into his veins before the Games, so his tissues were getting far more oxygen than the rest at that altitude, had been disqualified as well— and they had been his own cells, saved up for months.

"Are they being kept from thinking of it?" May wondered.

"That doesn't sound like him," Toby said. "There is another possibility, and if I'm right they're being awfully discreet. They may have thought of it, got hold of an MRI, and done a test run. If they did, they'd have found that *everyone* was saturated with nanos."

"I wonder why nobody else has said anything."

"They don't show up on normal settings. What I wonder is why nobody's noticed—" He got out his phone and did a search. "Ah. Nobody's doing PET scans anymore. The nanos must glom on to radioactive atoms to absorb all their output. Ha, that's another reason Connors couldn't be executed! They grabbed all the excess potassium to sort through it! And it hasn't shown up since then because they don't use that anymore. Just strap you down in a chamber full of sponge lime to soak up all the CO_2 you exhale, and as the oxygen runs out, you fall asleep and don't wake up."

"Who, me?"

"Behave."

"Who, me?"

"Good point."

May was silent for a few moments, then said, "I wonder what the next Olympics will be like. When everyone's learned how to reach their absolute limits. They will learn, you know."

"I'm wondering what this year's election will be like. How many people vote the way they do out of spite, do you think?"

May's face went blank, and she got out her phone and did a search herself. It took a while. Finally she said, "I can't find any smear ads."

Toby felt his jaw drop.

"Or panic ads. And that's with an asteroid coming in . . ." She checked something else. ". . . and the turnout at the primaries so far is low. Lower than usual." She did another check. "Toby, the largest turnout is Libertarian. They don't vote *at* other people. How did you know?"

He shrugged. "I'm an extrovert. I pay a lot of attention to people. —Behave," he said as she grinned and opened her mouth.

She closed her phone, then grabbed it out of the air as it suddenly rang and startled her.

"Nice save."

"Thanks. Good God, it's Sam Berlioz. —Hi, Sam, how in the world did you get my number?" There was a long wait, then she said, "I guess nobody else is likely to, then. What's up?" After an even longer wait, she said, "I see. Thanks, Sam. How you doing?" As she listened, her expression went from concerned to pleased, then astonished. Finally she said, "Wow. Keep me posted, will you? I like hearing from you. And thanks again." She signed off and said, "Samantha did the software for us. Hacker, crypto fanatic, so the phone call's secure. We hired her out of prison. She says there's a woman asking questions about me. Sam's young again, and pregnant. So's her co-wife. Their husband is chief of engineering at Andes Motors, incredibly smug, and exhausted, as you may imagine."

Ordinarily Toby would have been deeply and pruriently interested in details of the arrangement described, but at the moment he had higher priorities. "What kind of questions?"

"Questions about what Wyndham Launch had wanted to do next if things hadn't gone sour. Alice Johnson. Looked Arab but dressed and talked American. Didn't flash any ID, but she sounded Federal. Sam pointed her at the old Web site, and came on to her when she persisted, and she went away. Said Johnson looked angry when she made the pass, but not angry at Sam. You didn't even leer when I said her husband was exhausted."

"He's running errands for *two* pregnant women. I wasn't an only child, you know. How'd she get your number?"

"Worked out a list of possibilities for what my new name might be, by remembering everything I'd ever said to her, then went down the list hacking systems until she got a phone number. Her memory was always incredible, but now it must be perfect."

Toby winced. "I'm not sure I'd want to be a kid in that house. —What am I saying? No kid is ever going to get yelled at for trivial reasons again. Not twice by the same person, anyway."

May's eyes widened. "I already thought Connors was playing God. Now I'm not sure he's playing."

"I am," Toby realized. "But he's not playing God. He's just playing."

XVII

And a rock feels no pain.
And an island never cries.

—PAUL SIMON

1

Alice Johnson—she'd had her name changed to antagonize her family—had been mutilated as a little girl, to prevent her from "committing adultery with herself." It had the effect of making her a fanatically dedicated pursuer of terrorism. It also made her need to take a tranquilizer every time someone came on to her. After questioning Berlioz she meant to return to her hotel, but she decided to look in on the Games first. Her ID got her into the U.S. section of the Village, and persuasion got her to the field as the shooting competition was starting.

It wasn't what she'd expected, but she did approve: this year, before shooting, the competitor had to assemble a standard bolt-action rifle. That was timed, too.

JNAIT lost its first gold in that event. Their man was the most accurate, but the Switzer got his rifle together a lot faster than anyone else. Another Indian came out to talk with the dismayed man, and after a minute or so they both went over to congratulate the winner, who looked astonished at their doing so. The two shooters went on talking as they went to take the winners' stand, and the other man came back past Alice. He stopped, turned, and said, "Alice Johnson?"

She jumped slightly. Wishing she was armed, she said, "Have we met?"

"No. I saw your picture on the Al Jazeera site, way back when you had your name changed. I consider you a remarkably cool person. Mycroft Yellowhorse." He stuck out his hand.

She'd missed the events, but knew the name. "Fastest Man Alive," she said, shaking it.

He grinned. Perfect teeth. "So far. Chill suits are going to catch on. Are you expecting trouble? Last I checked you were a terrorism analyst."

"You a spy or something?"

"Nah. I might be a stalker if I could spare the time. I like being around cool people. There's a question pending."

"Oh. No, I'm just looking for someone to help with something."

"In Ecuador? Launch systems. Something to do with the Big Bad Rock, then."

"You sure you're not a spy?"

"I don't take direction that well. May I offer a suggestion?"

She shrugged and nodded. "Can't promise to take it."

"Fair enough. Get a budget and make a bid to the next person you talk to about it. The launch business is a *business*. The private sector just wants results. I have another suggestion: while you're here, take a shower as soon as you get out of bed, even if it's just a nap. It's not that hot at this altitude, but equatorial sunshine is brutal. I hope to see you again when you're feeling better." He nodded, turned, and continued to the JNAIT benches.

He seemed like a nice guy. Observant, too. Most of how she felt was residual stress from the pass earlier, but sleep and a shower were what she needed for that anyway.

She went back to the hotel room—one of thousands the U.S. government, like most, kept available in major cities all over the world for just such sudden visits—took a pill, watched "news" items about the Big Bad Rock—mostly clips from disaster movies—until she felt drowsy, and slept until the middle of the night.

She awoke ravenous, ordered from room service, stepped into the bathroom for a quick wash, and yelled in amazement when she discovered she was whole again.

2

As Forge finally got around to its final approach to Earth, the supply of oxygen began running low; just about all the rock outside the hot core had been converted. This was as expected. Accelerator tracks had been built to use specks of silicon as reaction mass. The trouble with that was, Earth was surrounded by valuable property, and the specks would go through anything in orbit with terrible effect. Therefore they had chosen a course that would allow them to aim the silicon exhaust outside geosynchronous orbit when they changed drives, keeping a maneuvering reserve of oxygen for rendezvous.

None were concerned that this put them temporarily on a collision course. There would be plenty of time to steer clear.

And there was no reason for anyone on Earth to be worried. Surely it was clear that the entities would not choose to destroy themselves.

XVIII

You furnish the pictures and I'll furnish the war.
> *—WILLIAM RANDOLPH HEARST*

On Sunday, Toby found out what *Lowdown* was. It wasn't an altogether awful experience, at least once the segment on the DHS arrests began.

Lowdown was run in accordance with the finest traditions of broadcast investigative journalism: scrambling the faces and voices of rumormongers to protect them, followed by ambush interviews of overworked desk jockeys, conducted by someone with the kind of voice God would have if God had a bigger ego. It was all Toby could stand to wait it out with the show in a corner of the screen, sound turned low. "*This* is why I don't check the news," he told May, as they watched yet another shot of someone running away from the camera.

She didn't have a direct answer. "Don't you want to know what Connors is doing about it?"

"I did. Now it feels like I'm slowing down on the way past a wrecked school bus."

They were silent until the part they wanted came on.

It was called "Chicken Big."

The title was the politest part of the segment.

Standing before a grim-looking building, anchor-man Arthur Fahy sternly informed the world at large, "Attorney General Stephen Wellman has determined to his own satisfaction that the Briareus Project, a nanotechnology-based mission sent out to the asteroid belt twenty-five years ago to bring back enough wealth to make everyone on Earth rich, was actually a terrorist plot. He has ordered agents of the Department of Homeland Security to arrest all the people who were involved in the work—at least, everyone who hasn't died of old age since then. Most of them are pensioners and can't afford a lawyer, and were being held incommunicado until we stepped in to provide them with representation. The DHS has described them as uncooperative, but we've found all of them to be willing to talk to someone who isn't threatening them."

The picture cut to a tiny, elderly Oriental woman with thin white hair. Toby was shocked to recognize Josie Bartlett, who'd done most of the primary work of translating electronic code into rod-and-gear mechanisms. She was sitting at a table in a little room, of the sort immediately recognizable to anyone who watched TV shows involving lawyers. Just past her on the screen was a very large, stern-looking man in a deep gray suit, who might have been brought in to represent her, or might have been casing the place for a covert-ops raid to spring her—or both; he looked like the sort of man who might have a tattoo on him somewhere that said DISPLAY ADAPTABILITY. The interviewer was offscreen to the left, and Josie glanced away from him to smile bravely at the camera and raise her hand for a shaky wave at the world.

Josie had once spent half an hour at an office party, before she finally cracked up, convincing Toby that she had come up with a method to allow the nanos to engage in sexual reproduction. This should be good.

Fahy's voice asked her, "Do you mind telling us about your situation?"

Josie smiled warmly and said, "Honey, I'm seventy years old and I like people. The only problem you might have is getting me to shut up."

"Do you know why you've been arrested?" said Fahy.

"In what sense?"

"Excuse me?"

"Well, there's more than one answer. One way to look at the situation is to just quote the charge the DHS came up with, high-tech terrorism, which basically means building something that they can't be bothered to understand and wasn't illegal to build when we made it. Another way is to say I was arrested because somebody in the current administration decided it'd be good for the polls if they looked busy. Both answers have the same origin, though, which is that a bunch of bureaucrats with guns went into a panic and decided to find someone to blame for their hysteria."

(There was something about Connors that just seemed to rub off on people. Josie had worked with him closely.)

"Have you been well-treated?"

She smiled hesitantly. "I may not be the best person to ask. The body cavity search was the most entertainment I've had in ten years."

The commando lawyer turned his head to stare at her for a moment, then went back to glaring at the guards who were standing by.

"Had you asked for a lawyer before we got here?"

"Every day. Everyone I talked to. Including my cell-mates. They've given me three different cellmates so far, but they all act like some kind of federal person. They never actually ask what I'm accused of, like a real person would, so they can claim whatever I might say is admissible. I keep getting new ones. I don't think the ones I've had were very healthy. They all look sort of shaky, and it just gets worse as the day goes on. I give them advice about diet, mostly. I've had a lot of experience with that sort of thing, too. I let them know about that so they know I'm not just quoting soap operas or something." Josie started to say something else, and the image jumped to later in the interview. The man seated next to her was slumped a good three inches lower now. He looked sort of shaky.

Both Toby and May missed Fahy's next question, and part of the answer, which was drowned out by their appalled nervous laughter. The expiration date allowed for by human evolution is well before fertility ends. One consequence of this is that practically anyone past forty or so has at least a few medical stories that are not for the faint of heart. And Josie was seventy.

Josie was saying, "They can link up to deal with more complex stuff on the spot, rather than go back to the main computer for instructions. There's nothing in their programming that would allow them to destroy themselves, so they're either doing some kind of navigational maneuver we just haven't figured out yet, or there's been some kind of accident that screwed up the basic program in the computer. What we need is to get Toby Glyer in on this."

"Unfortunately he's been killed," said Fahy.

"And you can believe as much of that as you want. Even a government agency wouldn't be that stupid. It sounds like something someone cooked up to keep people from asking where he is. I wouldn't be surprised if he's in a Pentagon basement being questioned under drugs. Which is worse than useless, because drugged people aren't so hot at doing creative work, and that's what we need here."

"So you think the government got frustrated and arrested all you folks to put pressure on Glyer?"

"I hardly think it's the whole government. I'm pretty sure, say, a park ranger would just ask for help. This would have to be just a few people at the top."

"You think the *president* ordered it?"

"It beats the daylights out of me. But the attorney general certainly has to know about it. In which case, if they really believe this is a threat, then to threaten and antagonize the only other people who might be able to help with the problem is essentially an act of war against the United States of America, and Bob Foster should probably have Steve Wellman arrested for treason."

"That seems extreme."

"You mean, compared to locking up a bunch of old farts with no money who can barely get around, and claiming they're terrorists so you can force them to work for free?"

The camera view cut to a walker in the corner of the interview room, then the screen switched back to Fahy outside the building. "Josephine Bartlett has had two hip replacements and reinforcing pins put in her right forearm. Another arrestee, Renee Dandridge, was employed by Watchstar as a cleaning lady, and requires regular medication to allow her to sleep without her lungs filling with fluid. Others have problems of their own. It's difficult to imagine such people presenting a threat. AOL-CBS is working to get the arrestees bail hearings, or at least have them moved to a facility where they can get decent medical care, but there's strong resistance from the Department of Homeland Security."

The next image showed a grainy view of Attorney General Wellman getting into his limousine, with a banner across the bottom of the screen that said LAPEL CAMERA. He was scowling out of the screen. "Aiding and abetting threats to the safety of this country is a crime. If you're not with us you're against us. Now stop questioning me or I'll arrest you as an accomplice."

Cut to Fahy outside the holding facility again: "A two-hundred-billion-ton meteor is getting four miles closer to Earth every second. The administration's response to this is, 'Don't ask questions.' And there you have it."

The next segment was "The Last Word," and was about the flammable propellants used in spray cans. Toby shut off his screen. May shut hers off. Toby said, "I wonder if we'll ever see Stephen Wellman again."

XIX

Where neither their property nor their honor is touched, most men live content.

—NICCOLO MACHIAVELLI

Alice saw *Lowdown* that night too. She didn't expect Wellman to be disappeared. She expected his deputy, Lisa Frost, to take over as AG when he retired for reasons of health. She started a security search of May Wyndham's records and went to bed.

On Monday morning, Alice checked the results, then sent a message to May Wyndham's old e-mail address. It hadn't been used to send anything in years, but it had been a lifetime account, so she might still look in on it.

Subject: **Launch system needed.**

I work in DHS intelligence. Not all of us think the job consists of locking up people who object to us locking up people. The people at the National Appointee Sinecure Association are busy making the universe safe for robots, and we need something to get to the Rock before it gets to us. If you

can help, I can get this approved as a Homeland
Security Goal Project, and *you will get paid.*
RSVP.
Alice Johnson

That done, she went to the Games again and hunted
up Mycroft Yellowhorse. She hadn't been able to get a
number or an e-mail for him at all.

The Indians were friendly, unless someone called them
Native Americans, in which case there followed lec-
tures about marginalization. (As a Wheaton-born third-
generation U.S. citizen of Kurdish ancestry, who kept
being called "Arab"-American, she had no inclination to
do any such thing; they got along.) They did seem to have
helpful intentions, but that was about all they had.

She asked a boxer, who'd just knocked out the Bulgar-
ian heavyweight four seconds after the bell, "Where can
I find Mycroft Yellowhorse?"

He grinned. "Unless you catch him at breakfast, you
can either wait until dinner, or look for a cloud of dust.
That'll be where he was last."

She told a woman in wrestler's tights, "I'd like to get
hold of Mycroft Yellowhorse."

"Who wouldn't? —Try the judges' box. He likes to go
grin at them."

She got to the cordon around the box and called out,
"Mycroft Yellowhorse?"

Several people looked frantically in all directions,
then turned to glare at her. A security man said, "You
might try the arcade. They blanked the high scores again
last night." He was smiling faintly. Interesting.

She rented a cart to get to the Village shopping mall, which she hadn't seen yet.

She never did get to see all of it. The size record had once been held by a mall in Canada, but even West Edmonton didn't have *two* Baskin-Robbinses.

After half an hour or so, and repeated checks of the numerous standing maps, she found the arcade, which was on a floor she'd missed before. She plugged in her cart outside it, ending the rental—there were plenty more when she wanted to leave—and went inside.

Her first thought was that she should have kept the cart. The arcade alone was about half the size of one floor of a normal indoor mall.

Her second was that the proprietor was a genius. Every kid who had been dragged along to the Olympics for purposes of cultural edification, and gotten fed up with watching sweaty people grunt, had come here. There must have been thousands. They all had somewhere to sit—even the ones who were waiting for a game to be available. The *snack bar* was essentially a regular mall's food court.

She headed for the snack bar, which was suddenly very appealing. It had been a long morning.

There was a crowd of kids around a Mastershot game. Other games had crowds around them, and the kids there were yelling when the player did well. These kids were quiet.

The player was a tall Indian with a long black braid down his back. He was playing two-gun mode, and shooting the guns out of the targets' hands while they were still drawing. The screen showed he had accumulated thirty-six free games. The number changed to thirty-seven as he shot the horns off a four-armed demon. Alice worked her way around until she could see his face; she knew who it was, but she wanted to study his expression.

He had none. He was just watching, firing, and watching some more.

The crowd's manner altered, many getting even more interested and nudging and murmuring to the ones who hadn't. She wondered what was on the screen now.

Yellowhorse blazed away at the bottom of the screen, then fired at something at the top of the screen, then raised the pistols. There was a loud wet crunching noise from the speakers, and all the watchers said, "Ahhhhh." He glanced at Alice and said something to a fat blond kid to his left. The kid's eyes bugged out, he nodded rapidly, and Yellowhorse gave him the pistols. The crowd applauded, and Yellowhorse raised his hands in acceptance and left the thirty-seven replays to the kid who'd evidently been watching longest.

He came over to where she was, looked around, and began moving toward the snack bar. People moved aside for him.

Once they were through both sets of doors it was quiet. "What did I just miss?" she said.

"Achilles," he said. "He's indestructible. It's a building site. You have to tear up the ground he's standing on so he can't use his speed, then drop a truckload of wet cement on him. After him it resets to level one. Come on, I'm rich, I'll spring for some pizzas."

"Do they have sushi?"

"Yeah, but I had that this morning. You go ahead, I'll

still spring." He waved at somebody, made some complicated gestures, and accompanied her to the Japanese section.

"I knew JNAIT was doing well, but how rich do you have to be to get *tired of sushi*?" she exclaimed.

He looked extremely pleased with her. "You must be a damn fine analyst," he said. "Not that rich. You do have to be able to afford it whenever you want, but you don't have to be Marcus Crassus rich. He said no man should consider himself rich unless he could raise and maintain his own army."

"So you're not that rich, then."

"Sure I am. I'm just saying you don't need to be. And it still takes a while. Pick and choose, the boats always include something weird."

"I can do weird."

He raised an eyebrow interestedly.

"I just mean I can eat stuff like blowfish."

The other eyebrow went up, and he smiled faintly.

She was starting to think she should have spent another day in her room. She turned to the counter and ordered a medium boat meal. She looked back and said, "Aren't you eating?"

"I already ordered. You don't have to know sign language in your job?"

"No, thank God. There's too much detail in my head as it is."

"Everything reminds you of everything?"

"Yes, exactly!"

He nodded. "Once you have your pension you should write."

"Hah. My pension is in U.S. dollars." The Mint had just started issuing five-hundred-dollar coins because it cost too much to print the bills, and the end was not in sight.

"Take a lump sum and immigrate to JNAIT."

"Retire to another country from an intelligence job? Not for long."

"They don't bother us. JNAIT has the Bomb."

She was horrified. "You realize they'd just slaughter you all if you destroyed a U.S. city, don't you?"

"What U.S. city? We made it very clear to the State Department last year that if they didn't stop their harassment we'd nuke *Mecca*."

Thereby starting total jihad. Islam worldwide had six times the population of the United States, and dynamite was cheap. "Jesus Christ!"

"I wouldn't count on it." He grinned like a carnivore.

Definitely another day in her room.

Which reminded her: "What did you do to me?"

"Not as— Order up."

He was evidently at least as observant as she was. They got to the pickup counter at the same time as her tray, which she looked at aghast. She was accustomed to sushi being a sliver of fish you could read large print through, on top of about a domino's worth of rice. This looked like some kind of international relief program. "This can't be mine!"

"Soup, salad, twenty assorted pieces—including one coelacanth, and a bakemono maki," he said. "It's what you ordered."

"Just wave and I'll bring your ice cream when you're done," said the boy behind the counter.

She'd forgotten about the dessert. "So you'll be here tomorrow?" she asked him.

He didn't get it, but Yellowhorse did and laughed. "Give it your best shot," he said. "You may surprise yourself." They headed for a table.

"If I eat all this at one sitting I'll turn into a blob," she said as they sat.

He poured her some tea. "That would astonish me excessively. You just won't get hungry for a longer while than usual."

She used wasabi and ginger and took a bite to give herself time to think of an answer.

She ate four pieces before she could stop long enough to speak. When she did, she said, "There's a question pending."

It was his own line, and he smiled. "I didn't do as much last week as you suppose. To give a more complete answer I'll need you to keep your mind open."

In the circumstances she was contemplating opening a lot more than her mind for him. "Could you hold off on the suggestive remarks, please?"

He raised that eyebrow again. "It didn't come out that way over here. The problem must be at your end."

After a moment's thought, she said, "That one was on purpose."

"Yes, it was." He smiled, and was interrupted by the arrival of a pizza that wouldn't have fit on her nightstand at home. It was accompanied by two quart bottles of milk.

He carded for them and began rearranging the bacon and pepperoni.

She spent a minute watching him meticulously ensure that every bite would have some of both. After some distracting thoughts about the precision of his hands, a connection was made in her head. "You're the one they couldn't find. Connors."

He looked delighted. "Damn, kid, you are *good*!"

"I thought what you did to me was some kind of enzyme thing until I saw you fixing your pizza. Nanotechnology has to be right the first time and never go wrong, doesn't it?"

"Right. We had to stop holding office potlucks because people were gaining so much weight. There were an awful lot of good cooks at Littlemeade."

"That was what Watchstar used to be called?"

"More precisely—" He looked at her to see if she got the mild joke, and showed a flash of disappointment. "It's what Watchstar bought out. Aside from people who worked there, there was only one investor in common with both. She wanted to be able to revive someone who was frozen after death. Third most beautiful eyes I've ever seen. I'm still working on that problem. *Lots* more details than keeping someone alive. As you say, it has to be right the first time."

" 'Third most beautiful'?" He kept a *list*?

"You have already called attention to the fact that I observe rigorous standards in some things." He uncapped a milk bottle, arranged a stack of paper napkins with the precision of a scrub nurse laying out surgical sponges, and started eating pizza.

It was searing hot and dripping oil, and he got none of the orange grease on his chin, his clothes, or anything but his fingers and the rest of the pizza.

He worked on the pizza with the dedicated resolve of a man with a commitment. She resumed eating her sushi.

She actually got that whole meal down without feeling gorged. He was almost done with his pizza, and she began policing the table. When he was done eating, he said, "You can smoke here, you know."

"I quit eight yea— how'd— the table. Yes. We pick up after ourselves." He was better at her job than she was.

He nodded. "We do. I quit in 2000. Lost a very foolish bet. Saved a fortune, though. —You know, this place should really be out in the arena."

"The snack bar?"

"The videogame arcade. Whole point of the Olympics is to show what your people can do in war. Thanks to the Japanese we've raised three generations of kids who can knock down a flight of nuclear missiles with their thumbs. It's certain to make a difference. —Now, as to your question: I sent a program to your bots. You were already saturated with them, like everyone else on the planet. Interesting that you figured out it was me."

"Post hoc reasoning," she said. "It was a miracle. You've been doing miracles."

He nodded. "Post hoc does work sometimes. —I had them leave your finger and retina prints alone."

"Good," she said nervously. "—Wait, you say everyone has them?"

"Goat Flu. It was a bot. Used virus shells for raw

materials. Now nobody's getting colds, herpes, AIDS, cancer, or any other viral infection. Plus, no more hay fever, and insects that bite you die. The bots also eat pollen and chitin. They don't last long if they dry out or get into the wrong pH, but they spread well enough by skin contact, and anybody with a cold or the flu sprayed them all over the place. I spent a few weeks at airport departure lines, shaking hands now and then with somebody who had the sniffles. Worked great."

"Do the bots have anything to do with why I'm so calm about this?" she said with sudden suspicion.

He shrugged. "Not directly. The fact that you're talking to a funny-looking, mostly white man, in his nineties, who was crippled from birth, but who is now a handsome Indian, a champion athlete, and young, may have had some influence on your thinking." He put on an expression of polite inquiry. "Could it be that your willing suspension of disbelief has been melted to slag?"

She had to laugh at that.

She thought hard about asking him a question, but decided to ask what she'd originally intended. "Can you get me in touch with May Wyndham?"

"Interesting you should think so. Tell me why you do."

"Nanotechnology. You must have known Toby Glyer, and he knew her."

"Not bad. ---I believe I could, but it would probably upset her. What do you need?"

"Something that can go up to that rock."

"By next month?"

"She was the best there ever was," Alice said.

Yellowhorse—Connors—looked at her for a long moment, then smiled in pure joy. "She was. I'll find out."

"What do I call you?" Alice said. "I mean, the different names—"

"Mycroft." He smiled again. "Mike."

"No, I like Mycroft. I'm Alice," she said, and gave the back of his hand a brief pat.

She almost fell out of the chair. For the instant of contact, she was filled with a sense of vibrant health and serene patience, both sensations far beyond anything she had ever imagined. He braced her arm and pushed her upright, a fistful of napkins between his hand and her skin. "You okay?"

"What just happened?" she said.

"In certain circumstances, a woman with a bot network can feel what someone she touches is feeling. I was sick for almost seventy years. Not being sick was a tremendous contrast, and the difference was very hard to get used to. Sometimes it recurs."

"It can pick up *states of mind*?"

"If I work at it, it can pick up whether or not you like your best friend's middle name. I've gone into someone else's head a total of twice. I regret both times. People have stuff they deserve to keep private, no matter how awful the people may be. Fortunately nobody else has that kind of control over the bots."

"What if someone learns?"

"They can't."

"Why not?"

"I'm not going to tell you. I designed them to prevent someone from turning the human race into willing slaves.

Whoever controls a communicable, linkable bot can do that. I'm the only person who I *know,* for a certainty, never would."

She got her head straightened out—mostly; giving up all of that calm assurance was like swearing off hot baths—and said, "Only women?"

He looked self-conscious. "Um. Yeah."

She felt her ears getting hot. She had a notion what those "certain circumstances" were. All at once she was amused and indignant. "So you just make women get horny whenever you want."

His face lost all expression. "Agent Johnson, I was sentenced to death for killing two serial rapists. Anybody can make one mistake. Don't call me a rapist again. Fair enough?"

"I never said you forced anyone," she said, startled.

"You said I compelled consent." He stood, took a step back, and said, "That's two. Initially it was nice meeting you. Good day."

"It's still consent," she protested.

He looked down at her, inhaled and exhaled through his nose, and said, in a low, even voice, "Try to listen just as you would if you didn't already know everything. It. Is rape. If the check. Bounces. Good day." He strode out past the counter, speaking to the cashier as he went by. She had to go around the table, and then collided with the kid bringing her ice cream. By the time she got up he was out of sight.

Just so the forces of destiny could screw with her gloomy mood, the ice cream was wonderful.

XX

The business of America is business.

—CALVIN COOLIDGE

1

Toby was enjoying the women's bicycle races, but on a
few past occasions in the course of her work, May had
genuinely found more interesting material while watching paint dry. She checked her old e-mail account, read a
surprising message, Lilithed the sender, thought it over,
and linked up to the system at their house. She'd down-
loaded her laptop files into it when they'd moved in.

Toby noticed. "Why so busy?"

"Sh."

Business. He nodded and watched the race in progress.

A good deal later, May said, "Someone from the DHS
wants to put up something that can meet the rock, and is
offering to pay for help. I'm having our system burn a
disc of some plans I made, back in the day. The Rukh
assembly line is mostly automated, and if they haven't
changed the core programs it should be able to turn out
the parts for our spaceplane in about a week. Another

week to assemble, and they can make the fuel while that's happening. The ship's all modules. —So who won?"

"I didn't notice. —Oh, stop grinning!"

May was saved from having to reply by the text light going on. It was from Connors, and said:

Alice Johnson from DHS says they need a space-plane. She is in Quito, and her personality defects do not include insincerity. Address is Hotel High Incal, room 429.

"The nanos let him judge *character*?" she exclaimed.

Toby shook his head. "He could always do that. Little-meade had some trouble with pilfering before he came to work for us. Really smooth job. He pointed Security at two people, they got caught. He never could explain how it worked. I think it may have just been that he pays complete attention to people."

2

At least she was out of the bathtub when she got the call. Alice wrapped herself in the hotel robe and tapped the Picture button, and the night manager said, "Ms. Johnson, there's someone here with a parcel. Are you expecting a delivery?"

He'd done it anyway. Fast, too. "Yes, send it up."

"She says she needs a signature."

"I'll be at the door."

She opened at the bell a couple of minutes later, and saw a hotel guard next to a pretty Indian girl in an ACME Delivery uniform. (She seemed to see pretty Indian girls wherever she turned lately.) The girl said, "Ms. Johnson? Signature here."

She signed and accepted a flat package, thanked her, closed the door, and had the seal open before it occurred to her that most, if not all, of those girls must be working for Yellowhorse. After all, *he* hadn't always been an Indian.

Or young. She wondered briefly just how old that "girl" really was.

Inside the package was a disc, with a note:

Aero Transcielo can follow the program, and they still pay me licensing fees. Just build the damn thing. Your problem is parasite control. Anyone wants his own improvements on it gets a bullet in the back of the head.

—Wyndham

Alice smiled. Now she really wanted to meet that woman.

She started her laptop and put the disc in.

Two minutes later she called Keith Danton, who she'd left in charge at home.

"—Yes, it's my boss, I do have to take this. —Yeah, Chief?"

"Wyndham's sent me a disc with a plan on it. It's a spaceplane. More cargo than both Shuttles put together, and there's a factory down here already set up to follow the blueprints."

"Holy geez, what'd you do, sacrifice a goat?" he said. "That's terrific! —So now what?"

"So now I phone the Director of Homeland Security and explain that getting someone to the asteroid will salvage the president's chance of reelection."

"You might not want to put it just that way. China launched something small this morning, and they've announced that they're going to put up more, assemble a ship in orbit, and turn the asteroid aside 'for the good of mankind.'"

Alice ran her entire vocabulary of bad words through her head and found none that were adequate. "And if they happen to drop it on India by mistake, 'oops,' right?"

"I was more concerned that they'll be able to get the rock into orbit, under their control—for a consideration. And my Mandarin's a little rusty."

Alice grimaced. Not conspicuously better for India, and a lot worse for everyone else. "Then we need to move fast. Talk to you later."

"Bye."

Alice disconnected, then used a phone number she was allowed to call exactly once.

XXI

By the work one knows the workman.

—JEAN DE LA FONTAINE

Emanuel Torres had been born on a farm uphill from Ibarra, at a time when everyone in the north end of South America had far too keen a consciousness of the concept of Lebensraum. Every day held the concern of looking northeast and seeing Venezuelan tanks rolling down the highway. Of course, they would have had to come through Colombia, but the television had made it clear that every Colombian who knew how to shoot was living in Los Angeles.

Then the miracles began.

The tanks had never come. The dictator had died of some minor ailment, which went untreated because he was certain that all doctors secretly worked for Israeli Intelligence, and Venezuela turned from militarization to exports of plastics and fertilizer. Those were cheap, and the farms all did better, and a trade school was built near Emanuel's home. Children were sent there to learn how to fix farm equipment. Emanuel turned out to have a talent with machines. He could fix anything that had ever worked.

And one day a tall blond angel from Heaven had come and asked him if he'd like to build spaceships.

He only had to work eight hours a day, and they fed him when he arrived, and he learned English, and there were the most marvelous things to read in English, and he built spaceships all week, and they *paid* him for all that!

They had paid him for that for almost thirty years now. He had learned more than he had imagined there was to learn, and he understood laminar flow and how a Coanda-Stine ambient athodyd worked, and why Gordon Wyndham had built the largest plane in history: half of its job was to make the liquid oxygen that went into the hybrid orbiters. Wyndham Launch had been bought by its employees and become Aero Transcielo, and when Emanuel suggested handing out astronaut wings for the tourist trade he'd gotten a raise and an office. He still spent most of his time on the line, but now he spent it teaching. He'd seen all the mistakes it was possible to make.

He did have to spend some time in the office every day. Once he had calculated that if all the documents he had had to deal with over the years were printed out on paper, a Rukh loaded with them would barely be able to take off. And that had been a couple of years back.

It was a rare day when he enjoyed spending time in the office.

* * *

He looked in on the Olympics while he was eating his lunch. The Indios had won some more gold medals, and once again everyone was acting like it was remarkable. It had never surprised Emanuel from the start. The Europeans had spent hundreds of years killing every Indio who was weak, slow, or careless.

Emanuel had also learned about evolution. By now some of the Indios were probably bulletproof.

That they had united and gotten rich made sense too. The disorganized ones and the poor bargainers had starved.

He finished eating, sighed, and checked his in-box.

The company had accepted contracts for two special orders. Both were manned orbiters. One was for the USA, and it was a design he'd seen when he'd been learning about the Rukh: a ship that could maneuver in space, land on the Moon, take off from there, and land anywhere on Earth that had a runway—or any long, reasonably flat patch. They also wanted a Rukh, so they could launch it themselves.

The other was for the Indios, and it was the same, but improved. Not by much. There wasn't a lot to improve. They'd paid in advance for triple shifts, and would be paying A-T to launch it for them.

The designs were in attached files, and they were in the line's programming format.

Emanuel left his office smiling. Today was a rare day indeed.

The angel was back.

XXII

One for all, or all for one we gage.

—WILLIAM SHAKESPEARE

Alice was assigned as Official Nagging Pest—
"liaison"—to the factory, since a) she was already here,
and b) Largo didn't want a routine-disturber like her
there.

(Good luck with that. If Keith's physical abilities had
matched his brains and inclinations, he'd need a hell of a
good secret identity.)

She stopped in once a day to see how things were going. She'd never imagined assembly-line workers could
be so jolly. People came by on their breaks to shake her
hand. One lady gave her a fruit basket.

There was a big banner across the end of the cafeteria
that said TRABAJE BIEN.

She understood the people at the factory after she'd
done a search on that. During NASA's Mercury Program, Gus Grissom, asked to address a crowd of employees at the plant that made the Atlas rockets, and
possessing all the oratorical ability of a man who had
dedicated his life to nothing but flying, had blurted,

"Well . . . do good work!" and been greeted with wild cheering.

These people understood the past.

And they knew they were building the future.

She'd spent a lot of time thinking about her conversation with Mycroft. She didn't figure out a thing until she did a search on the records of William Connors.

Birth name Guillaume Olivier Connors, but neither parent was French; good God, no wonder he'd changed it. It was a wonder he'd never brought a machine gun to school. Handwriting analysis suggested he'd spent a lot of time angry and frightened. Father started a successful employment agency, subsequently dissolving it, and several marriages, in alcohol. Mother was a wheel in the League of Women Voters—key delegate to the convention that nominated LBJ in 1964, later instrumental in pressuring broadcasters to remove "inappropriate content" from children's TV. Two older sisters. One did artwork for charitable organizations that all seemed to have a grudge against the country she lived in. The other had worked in the office responsible for censoring the language of federal publications, until someone looked a little more closely into a few accidents that had removed her superiors and gotten her promoted.

It appeared that William, a fanatical convicted killer, was the most reasonable, rational person in his family.

Married thirty-five years. Arrested in year fifteen, domestic violence. Pled guilty, suspended sentence, probation and one year compulsory counseling. No record of relationships after his wife's accident in 2018.

Connors's employment records showed he had done superior work at every job he'd had, but lost all but two due to excessive sick time. One of the ones he had kept was at Littlemeade Operation Systems. The other was right afterward, at the renowned Goldmine Promotions . . . which had been a shoestring operation called Curry Advertising until shortly after he showed up.

Never registered in any political Party.

A rather important detail of his arrest report had never been admitted into evidence at his trial, nor mentioned to the media: twenty-two bullets had been dug out of him after he was taken in. Three from his head. The NFR agents had certainly reloaded.

The judge had ordered him gagged after he refused to stop exclaiming, "A hundred and six!" while the agents' records were being read by the prosecutor.

An exhaustive side search showed Alice that a nine-year string of rape/torture murders with identical MO had ended just about the time of his killings. The murders—106 of them—had occurred all over the continental U.S., about one weekend a month, and two extraordinary details had never been noted before she checked: all the forensic evidence had been "lost" in each case, and no computer analysis of criminal activities had ever linked them together.

One of the dead agents had been a high-clearance computer analyst.

The inescapable conclusion made her throw up.

She rinsed out the wastebasket and then her mouth, and kept looking.

In prison, Connors had organized fantasy-gaming groups; tutored other prisoners in reading, science, and literature; stopped fights by talking spree killers out of their wrath; and organized an ongoing blood drive called Blood Brothers. It was still going. He himself had donated over thirteen gallons by the time he was pardoned.

An awful lot of incorrigibles had suddenly died in violent convulsions while he was there, starting about a year after his sentence was commuted. The rest of the prison population was the healthiest group in any federal, state, or local facility. A few new prisoners in Lee Ultra still dropped dead sometimes, and the rest were still healthier than was at all reasonable—including inmates who had been HIV positive when they came in. This dated back well before the disappearance of AIDS everywhere else.

A weird thought came to Alice, and she looked up the judge and prosecutor in the Connors case. Both had died in courtrooms. In violent convulsions. Not long after returning to work following surgery.

She checked personnel records for the DHS, and as an afterthought the BATF. Since 2030 there had been a gradual and steady increase in medical retirements among agents who had had surgery. The phrase "idiopathic neuralgia" came up a lot.

Since November of 2051, those cases had not been limited to surgical patients, and had increased to the point where the standard medical retirement procedure now included a security investigation. A few interesting things had been found, none of them involving leaks. Cover-ups, yes.

She did some more checking. Over the past couple of decades, more and more people who had gotten transfusions had become dedicated donors in turn.

He'd saturated the blood supply with nanobots. Then he'd made them contagious, and people called it Goat Flu.

Goat?

She did a search on goats.

They appeared to be going extinct. So were sheep. They'd quit reproducing.

The standard of living in places that used to rely on them was increasing. People were farming instead of herding.

They were able to farm because arable land was no longer being grazed down to bedrock. Deserts had stopped spreading.

And something like six hundred million people had died since November, of what WHO was calling Goat Flu syndrome (because it was worst in places where the sterility of goats had a major economic effect), and *no news source had been screaming about it.* None of the usual career alarmists had made political or financial mileage out of it—but several hundred had died of it.

The symptoms were easily mistaken for strychnine poisoning. Agony and bone-breaking convulsions.

There were no figures on Goat Flu syndrome deaths in China, but she had to wonder. She called up a NOW map of progress in women's rights, inverted the pattern, and compared the result to the WHO map. The maps were just about identical.

It is rape if the check bounces.

Treating women as property was a death sentence from which there was no appeal.

He was saving the world.

On a case-by-case basis.

Alice went back to the arcade again, looking for Mycroft Yellowhorse.

She'd been a loner growing up, and didn't have much experience with the society of children. She'd never known kids could be so good at stonewalling. If looks could kill she'd have been thin vapor. She persisted until she found one little blond girl who was willing to chat . . . at first. An older girl saw them talking, came over, showed the younger one her phone cam, and walked on. The girl she'd been talking with said, "You're the one who made him go away!" Then she kicked Alice in the ankle and ran off.

It was an enthusiastic and precise kick, right where the corner of a dresser hits on the way to the bathroom in the dark, and it hurt like a really big bastard. Alice sat down hard, clutched her wound, and screamed, *"God-dammit, I wanted to apologize to him!"*

She checked under her fingers, stared as the gash began closing, and heard, "Cross-country bicycle."

Alice looked up and saw the girl with the phone. She looked Oriental-Polynesian, and would have been amazingly pretty if her expression hadn't been that of someone who was deciding whether electrodes would be required. "I'll get him to come back if I can," Alice said.

The girl noticed Alice's ankle. Her manner changed. "Maybe you're okay," she said, face neutral. "You know how many gifted kids have died of abuse and neglect so far this year?"

Alice tried to follow this. "I'm afraid I don't."

"*None*," the girl said. "Don't waste his time. We look out for our own." She turned and walked into the crowd, which opened for her and closed behind her.

Alice stared after her as she absorbed this. Then she looked around.

A lot of kids were looking at her, but she spotted at least eight who were *observing* her. Boys, girls, big, little. They all had the same look to them. It was one she knew from the mirror. They were survivors.

The cross-country bicycle course was some way from the arena, and rough enough to make some future Olympic venues unlikely to be able to equal it. The start and finish were nine kilometers apart on the map, but the straight path held rocks and gullies. The route that wound between all the obstacles was twenty-five kilometers, but the rules allowed for shortcuts over bad terrain. The goal was to get from start to finish in the shortest time. Helicopters held judges and cameras to watch for fouls, and medical crews for accidents, but any course was fair game as long as you stayed with your bicycle; climbing a rock and hauling your bike after you on a rope, for instance, was an immediate disqualification.

Competitors started out at one-minute intervals. Mycroft Yellowhorse tightened the straps on his pack, turned aside from the path the general mass had taken, and set out on the straight-line route. A helicopter followed overhead.

Enthusiasts would have talked about the charges up steep rock and leaps over gullies for years, if not for the event at what came to be called the Big Gap.

About two klicks short of the finish, Yellowhorse got to the edge of a span six meters across and five deep and stopped.

Everyone watching him onscreen stopped breathing.

He turned away, and all over the world his adherents moaned.

He got about ten meters away, got off his bike, undid some extra straps on his pack, bound the bike to his back, and charged.

He landed a couple of meters past the other side of the gap, unstrapped his bike, took it back to the edge, got on, secured the loose straps, and rode the rest of the way without further incident.

Alice had been watching on her phone, at the finish line. The significance of his going back to the edge had not been lost on her. There were shortcuts where riders needed to walk their bikes, but they had to ride wherever possible. Otherwise—just to pick an example at random—someone incredibly tough and powerful could just pick up his bike and run in a straight line to the finish.

He'd even ridden back a greater distance than the width of the gap before jumping it. He'd covered the full distance, riding. He was playing fair.

He crossed the finish line just behind a Quebecois who had started fifteen minutes ahead of him.

He parked his bike next to the others, took off his pack, took out a lock, chained up the bike, peeled off his shirt, and held out his arm to the nearest IOC medic. The man had the testing gear out already. He tied off the arm, inspected the inside of the elbow, and looked the Fastest Man Alive in the eye with comical amazement. "Where's the mark from last time?"

"All better," Yellowhorse said.

The medic took three vials instead of two this time, not explaining why.

"A cheek swab works better for DNA testing," Yellowhorse said. "In case of bone marrow replacement or whatever."

"Didn't bring one," the man muttered, undoing the rubber tube.

Yellowhorse opened his pack and took out a first-aid kit. "Got one here," he said.

"Just get over to the stand," the medic snapped.

Alice was already heading that way.

When they met there, she said, "It took me a while to realize I didn't know what I was talking about. I'm sorry."

"Well done," he said. "Most people go a lifetime without figuring that out once." He held out his hand to shake.

She took it. It was just a handshake. She looked at her hand, frowning, wondering what was different. Then she realized: she wasn't horny this time.

"And now you've figured it out twice," he said as the flush crept up from her neck. "JNAIT doesn't post competitors' names before an event. How'd you talk one of the recovered around?"

"Said I wanted to apologize. Screamed it, really. I was sitting on the floor with my ankle bleeding from where a little girl kicked me."

"Blonde?"

"You know her?"

He shrugged. "Most likely. Don't know which one. Yellow hair and pink skin means a lot of Neanderthal genes. They were nocturnal cannibals. Cross that with farsighted hunters who chase down mammoths in packs, and you get the most aggressive creatures you can see without a microscope. I'm convinced the original Americans, forty thousand years ago, were near-pure Cro-Magnon, trying to get away from the crossbreeds. Worked for a while. Also explains why everyone was traditionally afraid of half-breeds. They had no resistance to that vicious European strain."

"The wound closed up while I watched."

He nodded. "When I see an abuse survivor I deliver the upgrade as soon as possible."

She studied his eyes. "You look out for your own. . . . They miss you. I said I'd get you to go back if I could."

He nodded again.

What the hell, her face was already red. "You want to go to my place?" she said.

He smiled. "Well, I'm not gay, blind, or stupid, so of course I do. But you'd be better off with somebody else. A partner who can commit. I'm waiting for someone to come back."

She got it in one. "Gabriella Campbell. You believe in reincarnation?"

"Not really. But she did."

She blinked fast to keep from crying. It was the most romantic thing she'd ever heard in her life.

"I always doubted the whole karmic debt thing, myself," he went on. "Seen too many kids like us. We can't all have been Hitler."

"We could all have been mothers," she said sourly.

He swayed, stared, and said, "When were you born?"

"Uh, July eleventh, 2019. Why?"

"You have any cats?"

She flinched. "Not anymore. I can't take them getting old and dying."

He nodded again, wincing himself. "I hear ya. You like vampire movies?"

She made a face. "Just the really old ones. Christopher Lee, Chris Sarandon. Oh, and Frank Langella."

"What do you think of Vlad's impalement hobby?"

"I think he spoke the same language as his enemies, only louder. Where are we going with this?"

"Well," he said, "once I get through with an awful lot of work, quite possibly your place."

"You think I'm your wife back from the dead? Are you crazy?"

"Of course," he said. "Is that a problem?"

Alice opened her mouth, paused, and finally said, "I have to think about it."

XXIII

Cowardice, as distinguished from panic, is almost always a lack of ability to suspend the functioning of the imagination.

—ERNEST HEMINGWAY

1

As Forge began maneuvering for rendezvous, a powered object approached from Earth. Broadcasts had said China had been assembling something in orbit, and this was it.

It massed a little over twenty tons, but it was small enough that there couldn't be room for a human inside.

It wasn't slowing down, either.

As it got closer, it came apart into two sections. Most of the volume was in the section that came ahead of the rest, though the masses were about equal. When that was halfway between Forge and the smaller part, the large part burst open, releasing a fine white powder.

Spectroscopy showed that to be boron trioxide. Barring unforeseen circumstances, it would be deposited along the sunward face of Forge.

Forge immediately directed the silicon exhaust at the small object that was following the powder.

The lesser module detonated with a force of just under a hundred quadrillion joules. The blast was rich in neutrons, and almost a fifth of them were directed in a narrow cone toward Forge. Some of the boron in the dust absorbed neutrons, emitted beta rays, and became carbon. The powder became incandescent and dispersed at great speed. Had the powder been in contact with Forge, and the detonation been closer, it would have caused enough recoil to push the asteroid into an orbit that would make rendezvous impossible.

It would also have destroyed most of their artifacts, and about half of Forge's population—killing vastly more intelligent life forms than currently lived on Earth.

The entities were seldom in full agreement about any course of action.

On this occasion there was no dispute.

2

There are people who, when the opportunity arises to get a little more sleep, can go back to sleep.

Toby Glyer was not one of those people.

May Wyndham was.

Fortunately, he *was* one of those people who could get around quietly in the morning. If he died and started haunting a house, nobody would ever know it. May, on the other hand, tended to navigate after rising by zero-range sonar: collide, then turn. It worked out, though, at least after Toby started taking the time to move stuff out of the way when he got up.

His phone began slithering across the counter while he was cooking breakfast. He wished he'd been given one with rubber backing; the effect when set to vibrate was downright creepy. Toby checked the caller ID: Yellow-horse. "Hi," he said quietly. "May's still asleep. 'Tsup?"

"China fired a twenty-megaton warhead at the asteroid. The bots shot it down. That was last night. In the past seven hours, every vessel of the Chinese Navy has had its stern perforated and propellers destroyed, and aircraft of Chinese registry have had their cockpits shredded. I got curious and checked satellite photos. They show a few thousand small craters laid out in very neat grids in various remote parts of China itself. Both of their orbital-launch facilities have also been restored to a state of nature. I think it was done with hypersonic crowbars. We need to speed things along down here."

Chilled, Toby said, "My God. They must be using the entire surface of the Rock as a telescope to be able to identify those. How many dead?"

"No comments made yet. I would think there must have been some, but in the case of the planes, at least, there was nobody in the cockpits at the time of impact. I may be the only one who's noticed that so far—aside from the Chinese, anyway. I can understand why they haven't said anything about that; entirely aside from making their intended victims look merciful, it is a damn scary accomplishment. —At any rate, the bots are denying China mobility and force. Ships, planes, missiles. I didn't think to check on their tanks until this minute. . . . Huh. Now that's interesting. Satellites show tank columns headed for the Russian border—sensibly enough—but some of the formations appear to be fighting each other."

"Civil war."

"I'd say so. —I wish there was another *term* for that. It always sounds like you don't shoot anyone you haven't been introduced to."

"The Chinese are traditionally very formal," Toby said, feeling a touch of hysteria.

"I find that remark simultaneously surreal and plausible. Brace up, slick. We have to make contact with the bots. They're ignoring ground-originated communications, they've clearly gone well beyond their original programming, and they have at least one good reason to be hostile. We need you to get into orbit and ID yourself to them."

"How in the hell—" Toby lowered his voice. "How are we supposed to do that?"

"JNAIT has a spaceplane almost ready to go. Just finished assembly two days ago, I paid for a rush job. Had the fuel made up and shipped here in April, right after Ecuador recognized us. Being installed as we speak. Suits are roughed out for the three of us, just need tailoring."

"Three? May?"

"She designed the thing. Can *you* fly a Wyndham 40-V? I know I can't."

May shambled into the kitchen like she might have trouble crossing a line of salt. "M'nin," she said, and yawned hugely. "'Zat?"

"Yellowhorse. He wants you to fly us all up to orbit in a spaceplane to talk to the nanos."

"Coffee first," she mumbled, and went to the steamer. As her cup was filling, she made a few odd smacking noises, frowned, and looked at Toby. "What did you say?"

XXIV

Ah, there are no longer any children!
—MOLIÈRE [JEAN-BAPTISTE POQUELIN]

1

The change came literally overnight.

It had been predicted by OB/GYNs months before; but there are ranks within the Brahmanism of doctors, and the baby-deliverers' status as performers of manual labor places them barely ahead of GPs. When they were not being patronized, they were simply disregarded.

It was first noticed by the rest of the medical profession in hospitals. One day the staff of the delivery rooms would be harried and frantic and making the usual annoyed remarks about conveyor belts; the next, there would be three babies born, hours apart, one of them overdue.

Various governments were swift to deal with the emergency by imposing useless, and occasionally lethally enforced, news blackouts of varying duration. All eventually dropped them in order to receive the aid money being collected to fix the problem.

Speaking on *The Sunrise Show,* special guest Turner Lexington, chairman of the Gaia Society, declared that it would be better for the world if the human race went extinct, and that the sterility was probably a planetary self-defense mechanism. He was beginning to expand on this theme when show hostess Rebecca Bloom hit him with a chair. Four hundred audience members—mostly women—later unanimously assured police that it looked like Lexington had been reaching for a gun.

Five days into the growing panic, a medical report was posted on the JNAIT Web site. Months earlier, the spike in false conception had attracted prompt attention in a nation whose entire adult population consisted, technically, of immigrants, and interested parties had been studying the matter for months. A statistical oddity had led to tests. These showed that the uterine wall of every woman examined had undergone a small structural change. The capillary-rich tissue that had formerly been sloughed off in menstruation was now resorbed instead, conserving nutrients. One consequence of this change was that the tissue was resistant to implantation of a dividing zygote. However, this resistance was usually—not always—temporarily suspended after a sexual climax. Tests, in which volunteers seeking to get pregnant were treated with the chemicals produced on such occasions, direct stimulus of the pleasure center of the brain, or both, had negative results. It had to happen the old-fashioned way.

And when it did, tissue receptivity lasted less than a day before wearing off.

Since the migration of a fertilized ovum from the fallopian tubes to the uterus could take anywhere from two to five days, the only women who were getting pregnant were the ones with extremely diligent lovers.

Even then, not all were successful. No medical condition was found in common among those who weren't.

It was a few more days before a USDA worker in Kansas noticed that there was no perceptible decline in births among the Amish there. Quick checking showed this to be true for the entire U.S. population of Amish.

The Amish, not much interested in the doings of the "English," had been unaware of the problem.

Once word got to them, they still weren't much interested.

However, Amish men did start manifesting a tendency, when dealing with outsiders, to suddenly smile for no perceptible reason.

2

The first thing Isobel Ross had done during her three years as president was to make Homeland Security a part of the Department of Justice. John Finch had planned to do it, but a dissecting aneurysm had interrupted his work. Finch's concern had been that, since its founding, the DHS had been slowly turning into Hoover's vision of the FBI. (Hoover had wanted the CIA to be part of the FBI, thereby creating an organization with powers of investigation and action at home and abroad. It would have given America its own KGB. Even Lyndon Johnson hadn't been willing to do that.)

The second thing she had done was have Finch's autopsy redone by an independent forensic investigator. The timing of President Finch's death had seemed just a little too convenient for the DHS. Nothing conclusive was found, but she'd replaced the top three levels of the DHS chain-of-command anyway.

The Director of Homeland Security was currently Tom Shake. Like all his predecessors, he was a vigorous supporter of everything about America except its principles.

God only knew how he'd learned about the JNAIT spaceplane; it wasn't like he read Alice's reports. At least, he'd made no response to anything else she'd put in them. As soon as he found out, though, he'd called her in the middle of the night to tell her she had to stop it.

"How am I supposed to do that?" she said.

"Any way you can. I'm sure you can think of something," he said. He was using the tone, instantly recognizable to any judge, that TV prosecutors used when they didn't want to be recorded authorizing blackmail and extortion when the cops had no grounds for a warrant.

She was already irritable from being awakened. "My grandparents were Kurdish, sir. Not Arab. Kurds have never really been into dynamite belts as a fashion statement."

"I would never suggest such a thing," he said indignantly. Now he made her think of a three-year-old whose face was covered in cookie crumbs.

"Then what *do* you suggest? Sir? Staging the suicide of the man in charge? Accusing them of child abuse, shooting whoever they send out to reply, and sending in a flamethrower tank when they shoot back?"

"I suggest you moderate your tone, Agent Johnson."

"Or what? You'll fire me and confiscate my pension? It ought to cover the cost of the stamp to mail my severance check. And for future reference, if you want deniability, mysterious phone calls after midnight *attract attention*."

"I was allowing for you being in another hemisphere," he said, in the patient tones of someone explaining something very simple.

"The *Southern* Hemisphere," she said.

"Exactly," he said.

"You might want to get hold of a globe. Do you recall the one in your office, sir?" she said.

"Of course. There's nothing wrong with *my* memory."

That did it. She abandoned what she'd originally intended to say, and exclaimed, "Excellent! Now, do you have any petroleum jelly, sir?"

Even he got that. After a pause, he said, "Agent Johnson, you are recalled to Largo for a disciplinary hearing."

"Great! It's a much better venue for the press conference I'll be holding."

"Any leak of classified information will be prosecuted as contrary to the public interest."

"Open review, of the mental competence of the man who's supposed to be protecting the U.S. from surprise attacks, is certainly in the public interest, and as an agent of Homeland Security, who is being blocked from going through channels by your bottlenecking critical information, I have no other recourse."

"You're fired. You will vacate your hotel room and return here to clear out your desk forthwith."

"If I'm fired, you're not giving me orders."

"You'll do as you're told if you want to stay healthy."

"You are now on record threatening the life of an American citizen. That makes you a terrorist."

"You— I have not given you permission to record me. You can't use it."

"You've forgotten the rules of the American legal system. You waived all rights and all expectation of privacy when *you* phoned *me*. Not only can I use it in court, but if I find someone silly enough to want to listen to you, I can sell copies and don't even have to pay you a share of the price."

"Don't try it." He hung up to prevent her from replying.

That suited her; she'd just wanted to make him be the one to hang up. She blocked his number, then called Mycroft Yellowhorse.

She didn't hear a ring before he picked up. "Hi, Alice. Ever had lobster tail sushi?"

It completely derailed her. "I never even heard of it."

"I invented it. You up for a midnight snack?"

"Uh, yeah, sure."

"Okay. I'll send a car. I warn you, it's huge—the sushi, not the car—okay, the car is too, but the point is, you won't move much for a while after eating the sushi. Bring whatever you might need later." He hung up.

Had he figured everything out, or had he somehow bugged and decrypted her phone so he knew what had happened? And in either case, come up with a cover story in case she was monitored.

She dressed, packed, and went downstairs to check out. There was a chubby Indian woman in a chauffeur's outfit waiting for her. "Ms. Johnson? Eva Ibarguren." She took Alice's bag as if it were stuffed with tissues, and turned to lead her to the car outside.

"I haven't checked out."

Over her shoulder, Ms. Ibarguren said, "I was told to

say, 'That's not your bill to pay.' I heard Yellowhorse say he figured you'd been fired."

"I was."

"What did you do?"

"Forgot to be tactful to an ignoramus."

The driver had to stop moving so she could laugh. "I meant, what was your job?"

"Encyclopedic analyst for the DHS."

Ms. Ibarguren turned back toward her, looked around with some care, switched the bag to her left hand, and said, "I'll go out the door ahead of you." She paused outside the door and looked around again, then said, "Stay here. I'll open the car. Go straight in."

"I hardly think they'd have me hit. Even if they would, there hasn't been time to set it up."

"I'm sure there hasn't. But if there aren't at least fifteen countries that would like to get hold of U.S. intelligence people, and who have agents in place whose jobs include keeping track of them, then I'm not on the same planet where I went to bed."

As Eva opened the car and shooed her in, Alice felt extremely foolish. Not for what she was doing; for not thinking of that.

Eva got into the driver's seat, locked up, opened the connecting window, and said, "You want a gun?"

"Best not. —Though I have been feeling kind of naked since I got here."

Eva gave her the once-over, smiled in an entirely unprofessional manner, and said, "Sorry to have missed that." With which she turned, started the car, and was all business, giving Alice time to recover from a case of severe self-consciousness, brought on by an utterly unexpected wave of curiosity.

She never had gotten an opportunity to find out what kind of partner she liked.

"If it helps, you can probably pick and choose from jobs in JNAIT," Eva said. "The information that people have to sort through always expands faster than search engines improve. It's a huge pain. A good reference librarian could name her price."

"I'd want to look over who I'd be working for," Alice said. "My last boss called me in the middle of the night because I was in another hemisphere."

Eva was silent for a while. Then she said, "D.C. is in the same time zone as Quito."

"I know. Not the sharpest knife in the drawer."

Eva said, "Sounds like he's not the sharpest *spoon*."

Alice began laughing, and as she did she felt a great weight drop away from her.

The JNAIT section of the Olympic Village had been redone by its occupants. In Art Deco.

Once she got over the shock, it looked great.

The flag had caused some trouble at the Olympiad. The old five-rings symbol on a white background had included at least one color of every national flag in the world up until 2051. JNAIT's flag was a gray calumet on a violet field. The IOC had, grudgingly, added a violet ring, and arranged the six at the corners of a hexagon.

She was still looking at the brilliant flag when she heard Mycroft behind her: "The tobacco pipe is better than my original suggestion. That was a copper penny with Dustin Hoffman's profile on it. Couldn't get permission from the estate."

Alice turned and put her arms around him.

His went around her, not as hard. Just as well, he felt like he could pick up a car and shove it through a wall.

After a minute she said, "Doesn't someone's image go into public domain after death?"

"So?" he said. "As far as I'm concerned, public domain is a crime against civilization. Patent and copyright should be nonsalable, permanent, and hereditary. They're the only form of nobility that is always earned. . . . Alice, on reflection I'm pretty sure you're not her."

She leaned back to look up at him. "I could wait with you."

He looked at her in wonder.

There really was lobster tail sushi.

The lobster had just finished cooking when she arrived.

It was incredible.

XXV

Hear the music, the thunder of the wings.

—ROBINSON JEFFERS

1

The scoops were complete. Objects in orbit around Earth had been charted, studied, and in case of doubt contacted. Anything that was working was carefully noted and allowed for. Armatures were deployed, film made ready to spread between them, and clusters of operators assigned to control the sectors.

Power storage was at full capacity. The entity population sorted themselves between the sections they would be staying with. Linkages were severed, and power was fed through the rails.

The section with most of the refined material was kicked backward sharply as the asteroid passed lunar orbit. The section with the hot core, and most of the mass and population, received a much milder push forward.

Forge moved ahead to swing by Earth and return to the asteroid belt, to catch and domesticate another Dinosaur Killer.

Foundry spread multiple wings of monomolecular film a thousand miles across, and dropped to make its first pass outside Earth's atmosphere, collecting the most expensive garbage in history. Holes opened and closed to avoid touching anything that was at all functional.

Even if it was Chinese.

China had enough problems at the moment.

2

While they waited for the suits to be tailored, May looked over schematics of the modified design. "Crazy son of a bitch," she said. Not unhappily.

Toby was dutifully checking the news. "What's he done?"

"Took out a damn heavy pump and an igniter and replaced them with a tank of peroxide. That'll react on contact with the aluminum carbide in the fuel. He's doubled the proportion of that, too. Bigger LOX tank, the lifter will have to cruise longer to fill it, but the exhaust energy goes way up. We could have done that."

"Why didn't you?"

"Too hot for the binder we were using. Trans-polybutadiene. Tough, but there was a chance it'd melt and start coming out in chunks. This guy just said 'screw it' and used linoleic epoxy. Basically all one molecule. I hate to think what he had to cast it in, some of it has to have reacted with the aluminum . . . good God, he used the aluminum carbide as hardener instead of polyamines.

And as an alkyl catalyst—well, pseudo-alkyl—for the olefin bonds."

"Boron trifluoride would perhaps have been a trifle too exciting," Toby conceded. Not to mention loud.

"So what's new?"

"Our people have been moved to one of the facilities that America's hardworking Congressmen have had built in case any of them get caught."

"I hope they like golfing. Otherwise, great. Anything else?"

"There's another Chinese splinter state." Chinese history was composed, in large part, of contests between warlords to see who could massacre more of the population, the winner being awarded the survivors. Multiple tank divisions shooting it out hadn't been enough to cause a general rebellion against the Mao Dynasty, but when the birthrate dropped close to zero, suddenly nobody had enough troops to round up the deserters going home to their families.

"That's five?"

"Six, if you count Tibet. Which Tibet doesn't. —This one's actually writing a Constitution. Capital's Kowloon. Briefly known as Hong Kong."

"Briefly?"

"Briefly for China."

"What 'Republic' are *they* now?"

Toby shook his head, grinning. "They're the 'Empire of Kwangtung,' and they've got an heir to the Ming Dynasty as Son of Heaven. Richard Chu. Software genius, Caltech. Before my time. Last year he was chief recordkeeper for the Hong Kong Director of Imports and Customs. He's already suggested a dynastic marriage between his great-granddaughter Julia and Martin Windsor. They're both fifteen."

"Which one's Martin?"

"Duke of York's youngest son. Quiet type, hasn't thrown up on any rock stars or anything."

"What, is he adopted?"

"He's got the Windsor nose. I'm thinking mutation. —Saw a story earlier about the DHS. Looks like the director got the same bug the attorney general came down with."

"Any idea how he picked it up?" she said dryly.

"Might have something to do with that guy they caught in the JNAIT hangar last week with all the magnesium powder. New director's someone I never heard of before. Keith Danton."

"Danton is not a felicitous name for a guy in politics."

"Well, as long as the Speaker of the House doesn't start channeling Robespierre—which I admit is not unheard of—he should be okay. —He's pulled everyone off random-harassment duty and aimed them at plausible suspects. Did an end run on the media uproar by announcing he was establishing a Profiling Division."

"Sounds sensible. This guy got appointed *how*?"

"Apparently by being the only one on the list who showed up at Attorney General Frost's selection meeting. Everyone else called in sick. Severe aches and pains." Toby cleared his throat. "Idiopathic neuralgia."

May bit her lips to keep from laughing, and finally got out, "So he got the job by having *none* of the qualifications of anyone else who ever held it."

"Seems as if. —Any more surprises on the space-plane?"

"What, you mean *aside* from little stuff like increasing the delta vee by about twenty percent? Yeah, I'm the pilot and I still have no idea what's in the cargo module. I wonder what unscrupulous character gave him that idea?"

"He did spend all that time in prison," Toby pointed out with a straight face.

May looked swiftly around the room, then said, "It won't help to put away all the magazines, I can take off my shirt and whap you with that."

"So my evil plan is working," Toby said.

May took off her shirt and whapped him with it.

Not much progress got made for a while after that.

May took shorter showers, so she got out first to answer the phone. It was Yellowhorse. "Evil Genius Enterprises, do you have an account with us?" she said.

"Last I looked I was the plurality shareholder," he said. "From your calm demeanor I gather you haven't heard the latest word on the asteroid. I just got an alert. It's divided. Most of it apparently went back for more rocks, but the smaller part spread a sail and swept a hell of a lot of crud out of orbit. It's decelerating pretty smartly. It'll have to take at least one more pass to reach a circular orbit. Maybe two, depending how low they intend to go. It'll be between one and two weeks. If it's going to LEO, the U.S. will have enough time to put up their bird." His voice dropped to the tone of the emcee of a Hallowe'en fair: "How are things in your town?"

Still reeling from repeated shocks, May said, "You might have had the decency to use a dramatic pause after you said it divided."

"Sorry," he lied cheerfully. "Want me to call back? I could open with 'Watch the skies!' And I played the soothsayer in a prison production of *Julius Caesar,* so I can do a *great* hebephrenic babble. Want to hear?"

"I'd rather eat a lizard."

"Well," he said, his voice now low and confidential, "I might know a guy."

May stood silently staring at the wall, mentally renewing her mighty oath to get the better of this man in repartee someday. She didn't resist as Toby took the phone from her.

"Hi, Mycroft," Toby said. "What did you say to her this time?" There followed a long pause as the entire conversation was repeated verbatim—which could be disturbing for an original participant to hear, as Yellowhorse would accurately reproduce timing and intonation. Toby had told her he'd always done that, too. She could follow the recitation from Toby's reactions: "Hch.... You're the general partner.... Huh! ... Heh.... Very thoughtful of them.... Oh geez, that's all we need.... Don't *do* that! ... Well, she's right.... As opposed to? ... You would. —Is that it? ... No, she's just opening a package from Haiti. Ordered this little wax doll. We already have a book on acupuncture." (May grinned and hugged him from the side.) "I assume most of the rest of the world is running around in circles screaming?" He nodded a few times, then said, "How should I know? They're your tailors. I think we're good to go when the rest is." He looked at May, who nodded. "Yep," Toby said. He nodded a couple more times in silence, then said, "Okay, see you at the hangar." He signed off, handed May the phone, and said, "Three days."

"Finally!" She gave him a smooch, then said, "What did he say about the world response?"

"I quote: 'The Pope disapproves, Russia has mobilized, Japan has gone on triple shifts, and France has surrendered.'"

She snorted. Then she said, "You didn't laugh at that?"

"I got too used to him. Besides, when he's On, you can't laugh because you miss the next three jokes."

"Yipe. That must have gotten awfully old."

"Now and then. The trouble is, the crazy sonofabitch puts genuine information into some of this stuff, so you can't just stop listening." He stopped and thought about what he'd just said. "Oh good grief." He went to the screen and switched it on. After some rapid keywork, he said, "The Vatican has denounced the 'attack' on China, Moscow is calling up reservists, Tokyo has passed another New Economic Plan in emergency session, and President LeFavre has announced his nation's willingness to work with the nanomachines to redress their grievances. He did it to me again!"

Trying not to laugh, May asked, "What did he say when you confirmed?"

"'Bring your towel, and put the fish in your ear.' Literary reference."

XXVI

All this and Heaven too.

—*MATTHEW HENRY*

"Fish?" said Alice. The odd random comments were getting obtrusive.

"Literary reference," said Mycroft Yellowhorse. "Douglas Adams." He did some things to the phone, but nothing that she considered sufficient retribution for taking them away from a limp drowse. Then he said, "They've got copies at the mall." He set it down, scooped her up, and carried her to the bathroom.

"We're stopping so we can go *buy a book*?"

"I don't want to use up my entire repertoire at once." He stepped into the shower and set her down.

"More of the same suits me fine," she said, and flinched unnecessarily as the water came on already warm. As he began lathering her up, she said, "Does that shared-sensation thing work when there's two girls with you? I mean, do they get it from each other too?"

He paused, eyebrows raised. "You're decadent after one day?"

"No, obsessive after thirty-three years."

"It wasn't a criticism. 'Anything done for the first time releases a demon.'"

"Huh?"

"Literary reference. Dave Sim."

"I know that name!" she said, pleased at having finally caught one.

He stood up straight, put on an expression of delight, and clasped his hands together by his jaw. Then he jumped and barked like a seal—she had grabbed. "No fair!" he said.

She let go. "He was on the Inappropriate list when I was in school. Misogynist."

"He wasn't," Mycroft said. "He was just walking wounded after a bad marriage. Some things you never recover from."

"Still in the denial stage?"

"Turn." He began washing her back. "I grew up with that Five Stages of Loss business. I consider all touchy-feely terms invalidating. It's like being a teenager and getting described as 'going through a phase' when you try to get taken seriously as a human being. 'Denial, anger, bargaining, sorrow, acceptance.' Know what their real names are? Shock, defiance, cunning, torment, and apathy. I grant you, the woman who originally named the conditions was just observing and reporting the phenomena she saw as best she could, and *she* was helpful, encouraging, and respectful. But everyone since then has tried to shove the bereaved along, like it was a procedure. That way they don't have to deal with them as *people*. It's why, ultimately, every drug prescribed for any strong emotion produces apathy. That's the desired condition of a nonentity."

"I think you may be overgeneralizing from your own history." They'd done a lot more talking than she'd expected. The bots had to be why neither of them had white hair yet. She wasn't sure when she'd turned red; they'd been distracted.

"I freely acknowledge that I am the sort of person who looks at those charming Currier and Ives prints and wonders how many inhabitants of the snowbound houses are, at that moment, being forced to resort to cannibalism. That being admitted, consider how the selfsame touchy-feely people have always refused to deal with what had been and was being done to hundreds of millions of little girls just like you." When she went rigid, he put his arms around her and said into her ear, "You never let yourself go past defiance. And you were *right*." She relaxed and leaned back against him. "You're wiggling," he presently accused.

"You obviously like it," she pointed out.

"You had *weeks* to take the edge off, you know."

She nodded. "And I did."

"This is what's *left*? Merciful heavens."

Later, out of the shower and toweled dry—the air-circulator arrangement was clever, but better suited to solo washing—she said, "I'm going to be worrying while you're up there."

He paused and studied her face. "You don't get dizzy

upside down," he mused. "The 40-V seats up to fifteen. I think we can fit a suit in three days. Sound interesting?"

"You want me to come?"

"Certainly."

XXVII

Every reform, however necessary, will by weak minds
be carried to an excess, that itself will need reforming.
— **SAMUEL TAYLOR COLERIDGE**

1

The amount of valuable material abandoned in Earth orbit was absurd, but what had been done about it, prior to Foundry's arrival, gave the entities a handle on the term "ludicrous." Monitoring of communications had revealed that the most capable of the spacefaring powers had actually enacted regulations that specifically required new objects to be designed to reenter and vaporize from the heat of atmospheric compression. The first enterprise to go up and collect the waste could have made itself rich in the extreme, but most of Earth's powers were participants in a council whose members had passed rules forbidding each other to engage in such activity—among many other activities whose only possible results would have been to improve human welfare. This seemed to be the council's principal function.

The entities decided that this was not their problem, and it would be a wasteful indulgence to destroy the meeting place of the council . . . for free.

Foundry, which was not a member of the United

Nations and not likely to apply, had taken up less than a quarter of the debris on its first pass. The second pass was slow enough to allow the oncoming material to be vaporized by lasers and the exhaust before it hit the scoops, which had been repaired by then. Deceleration during this pass put Foundry in an orbit whose period was slightly more than half a planetary rotation. There remained a good deal of eccentricity to the orbit, so the armatures were withdrawn, to process the new material collected on the scoops, and to simplify trim maneuvers.

2

The near-transparency of the suits, though he knew it was useful for the nanos, bothered Toby a lot more than it did May. "I look like a magazine cover from 1943," he said as they emerged into the hangar.

"Yeah," she said huskily, "Captain America."

It was true he was in better shape than he'd ever been, including the first time he was this young. That, and the way she was looking at him, made it suddenly easier to take. "You don't mind yours?"

"It's not like anybody's going to stare at me but you. I get to wear a classic working spacesuit. And I always *wanted* to look like a Kelly Freas poster."

"You're not wearing enough makeup."

May stuck her tongue out at him.

"You always know how to get on my good side," he said.

"You might have said something before you got your recycler connected."

He hadn't expected her to have an answer. "Ah. How's yours?" he said.

"Intensely personal, but it beats a catheter. —Sh!" she said, holding up a hand and looking grave and alert.

Toby stared at her, looked around, looked at her again, turned his hands up, and shook his head.

May pointed out of the hangar door at an approaching car. "Indians!"

Every now and then she cracked him up a lot more than she expected.

He got himself together as Yellowhorse got out of the car. After a moment Toby said, "No, *that's* Captain America."

"That's more like Superman," she said. On TV she'd never really seen how big Yellowhorse was. "And that's a Frank Frazetta poster," she grumbled as a woman got out after him. Both had suits on, but in their case the suits were decorated. Yellowhorse's, naturally, was done in streaks of war paint, but the woman's had the kind of tracery lingerie uses to make you uncertain of how much you're really seeing. "Hey, how come our suits don't get fancy designs?" she called out as they came in and the car drove off.

"What did you think the paints were for?" Yellowhorse called back.

"Paints?"

"In the patching kit. You didn't inspect your gear?"

"We just got this stuff on," Toby said.

"Oh. Well, we have a couple of hours before the first

easy launch window. —This is Alice Johnson, formerly DHS, now a security consultant for JNAIT. Alice, May Wyndham."

May shook her hand. "I wish my suit looked like yours."

"I think yours looks *great*," Alice said, looking it over with a smile.

Oh dear. "Thanks," May said.

Alice caught the undercurrent. "Oops. Sorry, I'll tone it down. I pretty much just discovered sex. Born Moslem. Clitoris amputated. Mycroft grew it back."

May literally staggered with the realization: "If he can do that, he can heal cripples!" she said, waving her arms for balance. Damn boots.

"That's who about a third of our immigrants are," Yellowhorse said as Toby caught her. "Were, anyway."

"Oliver Carter, CIA. You will all turn and raise your hands," called a man from a side door. He was white, armed, and wearing a standard gray suit and red tie, which at this latitude made him a lunatic. "William Connors, you are under arrest for sedition, rebellion, and treason." He had about twenty meters to cross as he approached.

Yellowhorse turned to face him, and said, "Alice, the man with May is Tobias Desmond Glyer." He drew a sharp breath, shuddered faintly, turned sheer black, and charged.

The boots didn't impede *him* at all.

Every round from the clip hit him. Then he hit the gunman, once, with a palm to the chest as he went past.

The Company man was flung aside into a stack of

empty packing cases, the only thing he could have hit that wouldn't have shattered his bones. He began hauling himself out of the mess at once to go after his machine pistol, but Alice reached him and stamped on his hand. He grabbed for her, ignoring his injury, and she leapt up and kicked him in the head. He fell backward, unable to coordinate but still trying to act. "He's drugged!" she shouted, and spun aside from the red laser spot on her face as a bullet whizzed by.

"Thomas Appleton Swift Pleasurizer!" Yellowhorse bellowed, and there were thumps and crashing sounds from several places in and outside the hangar. He came back over to the original shooter, who was now doing nothing except twitching ecstatically. Yellowhorse pried fifteen bullets from dents in his torso and arms, and said, "I thought I couldn't *go* senile. Should have done that in the first place. I *should* have realized somebody would hit on the idea of loading assassins with painkillers." He picked up Carter by the scruff of his collar, put his other arm around Alice, and came back over to May and Toby. The whole thing had taken about twenty seconds. "You're mistaken," he said to May. "It's not Superman who's transformed by saying the name of the wizard who gave power and purpose to a cripple." He'd heard her from the *car*?

"It turned you bulletproof," Toby said. That seemed to be all he had at the moment.

"Nominally. I've been shot before, it sucks. The thing is, he was firing sniper bullets: high speed, hardcase, denser than usual, and they would have drilled right through me and hit you folks. Fortunately I also made the suits tough enough to stop a glass knife. Don't try this at home. —I have quite a collection of bot triggers for various situations. Some verbal, some situational. Things I wouldn't normally say or do. Most don't work on people with the upgrade, some only work on me. —Alice, how do you feel?"

"A little sore, but I don't mind," she said.

There was a moment of silence. "You mean from wrenching aside to dodge the bullet," he said.

"Of course," she said, deadpan. "—I didn't break his neck, I figured you must need him or you'd have taken his head off."

"I most certainly would not. It's a disgusting sight. But thanks." Yellowhorse let go of her, took Carter by his shirt front, and said, *"Feel the burn."*

Carter looked shocked, then began to weep.

"Snap out of it."

Carter stopped crying and started to look worried.

"The rest of your team is still getting direct limbic stimulus. They'll be incurably addicted in ten minutes at most. Now tell me, why did you decide to risk World War Three by pissing off JNAIT?"

"We had people searching Mecca for months," Carter said. "They found the bomb."

Yellowhorse raised his eyebrows. "Do tell. Describe this bomb you found."

"A hundred and seventy kilotons," Carter said. "Did you think I was bluffing? I was given a picture to show you. Jacket pocket."

The picture was extracted and examined. "Well, this is disturbing," Yellowhorse said.

"I thought you'd see it that way."

"I doubt it. My warhead is in orbit. I've never seen *this* bomb before in my life. Now, go find your men and give each of them a big sloppy kiss. *Repent, sinner!*" He slapped the man on the forehead and turned him loose.

Carter staggered off to the far side of the hangar, looking stupefied.

"We need to find the guards they took out," Yellowhorse said. "Then we need to leave." He got out his phone and sent an automatic message, then led them outside, running. An ambulance siren started up in the distance.

As they reached the first man, May said, "That was quick thinking on the bomb thing."

"Hardly," Yellowhorse said as he knelt and opened the man's shirt. "Mine's two homemade fission imploders, each about Nagasaki yield. One fireball pancakes the other into the ground and scoops out a crater a mile across. Fusion is a lot of work. And this one's a government job anyway. *I gotta go feed my witch,*" he said, hands on the man's chest. The guard twitched, gasped, and started coughing horribly. As he looked around, Yellowhorse got out the photo and handed it to May. "This way." He ran around the corner of the hangar and found the next man.

"You can *raise the dead*?" Toby said.

"Lots of people can. Depends what you know and how dead they are."

"But you do it by talking to them."

"Don't be silly, they can't hear me. I quoted William Goldman to trigger *my* bots. Then they passed the word."

Four guards had each been stabbed from behind, through a lung so they couldn't call out, and left to drown in their own blood. May looked at the picture rather than look at the men. "Who put this one in Mecca, then?" she said, once he couldn't detect any more fresh corpses.

He shook his head. "God knows. The casing is French, so it could have been anybody. Hang on." The airport ambulances were just arriving, and he went to talk to the crews for a bit. He came back and said, "They'll be looked after. They're recent enough that the brain should still hold its connection settings pretty well. Let's get to our bird, shall we?"

"What about the spooks?" said Toby.

"The crews will take their guns and ID, but then I'm giving them a second chance," Yellowhorse said.

"Are you crazy? —Strike that. *Why?*"

"Because I am really, really pissed. Stone reminds me of the union rep at dear old William Golding High School, and his men weren't drafted. In less than a day they're going to be teenage girls who appear to have damn near no memory. Language and basic hygiene, and that'll seem to be about it. In fact they'll remember everything. They'll just be unable to express it to anyone. New prints, altered DNA, no identity. They'll be safe from abuse, but being taken seriously as human beings is a problem for another generation. Childhood is still its own punishment. I saved the men they killed, but it remains to be seen how much memory is restored. Karma's such a bitch."

"Yes," Alice said, "but she swallows."

Yellowhorse made a choking noise for a moment,

then patted Alice very gently on the top of her head. He led them back into the hangar, loaded their four equipment packages in the back of a hauler, and said, "This way, folks."

May got on, looked at the cluster of eight confused, frightened men, and didn't look at them again.

The Rukh they'd be using was in another part of the airport, in a *big* hangar, this one with a lot more people around. Some of the people had tools, others had cameras and were bothering the ones with tools, some had weapons and were interfering with the ones with cameras. All were ignored by the four.

The 40-V had been mounted the night before.

After a while Toby looked at May. She was still looking at the orbiter.

It was exceedingly beautiful.

In addition to the elegance of its design, it had been completely covered in a pattern of brilliant feathers, in every color that flame has. Along the nose on the left side (and presumably the right) was the word *Firebird,* in fluorescent violet.

"Wow," Alice said. "Mycroft . . . how did you know the bomb casing is French? Can you use your eyes like a spectrometer or something?"

"I could, but I didn't. It's too weird, and almost useless on any normal photograph anyway. —The numbers stenciled on it include two sevens, both of which have that superfluous little decorative line through them. This is on an object that's intended to be vaporized. Nobody else would do that. Nobody else would sell an H-bomb, either. I blame the wine and cheese. Always be suspicious of a culture whose cuisine is based on ingredients with no expiration date."

May, who detested wine and was at best lukewarm about cheese, turned her head to look at Yellowhorse. Then she looked at Toby.

"I said he had a position piece on everything," Toby said.

"You didn't say he was *right*," she said. She looked at Yellowhorse again. "Why didn't you ever write any science fiction?" she demanded.

"Good God, the same reason I never bought an elephant. As cool as it is, it still takes up all your time, and it absolutely cannot be justified by the return on investment. If I ever have to write again, I'll stick to romance novels, thank you."

"You who the what?"

He nodded. "It came to me when I was in prison. The only guy I ever saw shanked had torn a page in a romance novel. Shanked unfairly, I might add, as all the ones in the library were pretty worn out. —I was bored and broke, so I read a few and got the pattern down, then bartered some favors for time at a keyboard. —I had the advantage of having been sick for an incredibly long time, so I know work-arounds for all *kinds* of problems. As a side effect I became the go-to man inside. When I started to write . . . I need to tell you a somewhat obscure story. Let's get going, it can wait a bit."

They went to the elevator, waited for it to be rolled into place, and got in. Toby was fidgeting with impatience.

They plugged in their gear, put on their helmets, and found their seats, May and Toby in front. The cabin was cramped. "I left the controls the way you designed them," Yellowhorse said.

"Toby did say you planned for me to fly it," May said, powering up the screen for the checklist.

"Who else?"

"What if I'd turned you down?" she said.

"Well, the mission *is* dangerous, possibly foolhardy, and conceivably insane. And you're a test pilot. So it never crossed my mind."

Toby hurt his lips a little, biting them to keep his mouth shut. Fortunately May just snorted and continued her work without noticing him.

"The U.S. model was changed back to standard instrumentation," Alice said.

"That's going to slow them down," May said absently. "Is our cargo loaded?"

"It's in my pocket," Yellowhorse said.

All three of them turned to look at him.

"It was an idea I got from Josie Bartlett," he began.

Toby burst out laughing. "You're bringing them *broads*?" he said.

"Well, there goes that surprise. Yeah, they'll develop faster if they exchange modifications when they reproduce. These have the same kernel as your original design, iridium."

"Hey, that reminds me. What does Goat Flu use in the buckyball?" Toby said.

"Twenty atoms of carbon-13 framing a dodecahedron,

linked to twenty of the shell atoms. It's very stable." Diamond. It certainly was stable.

"Why . . . oh, of course, you have so much left over anyway." Minority isotopes were left out of nanos because they screwed up the balance.

"Yeah. —Oh, and the new ones get iridium-191 instead of 193. Rarer isotope. That way the guys will have to compete for attention. Tough selection, only about half will get partners."

"Not necessarily," said Alice, with a prim look that really didn't suit her manner.

"Cough cough," said Yellowhorse. "You set up, May?"

"Let me jack in. —Cosmos Traffic Control, this is *Firebird*. You ready to light this candle?" Only she heard the reply, but they all heard the Rukh powering up. "—Okay, crew, we'll be in the air in twenty minutes, then it'll be an hour to fill the LOX tank. Start talking."

"Wait," Alice said. "I never got this part. Why isn't it full now?" When they all looked at her, she was defensive. "I had other stuff on my mind growing up."

"It's not— Okay, it *is* rocket science," May said. "But it's not the really hard part. Without the liquid oxygen in it, the 40-V weighs as much as a fueled Rukh can carry. The LOX weighs substantially more than the fuel that's needed to get us to altitude and make the LOX. If we didn't make the liquid oxygen in flight, the orbiter would have to be a lot smaller. We could have made the 40-V even bigger if we had the Rukh start off almost empty and get refueled in flight, but the nose attachment would have cut the top speed of the Rukh, so all the extra weight would have to be solid fuel for the orbiter anyway."

"At more than twice the launch cost," Toby said.

"I was wondering when someone would mention money," Alice laughed. "Wherever two or more are gathered in the name of private space travel—"

"This ain't Need Another Seven Astronauts," Yellowhorse cut in, in a remarkably mild tone considering how Toby had heard him speak on the subject before. "We're not attention whores, we're not making the Universe safe for robots, and we're not boldly entrenching where no bureaucrat has entrenched before. The only reason to walk into the jaws of Death is so's you can steal his gold teeth."

"Is *what*?" Alice said, and started laughing again.

"Good God, you've never read Terry Pratchett either? Why are you here again?"

"Um, because I can get a knot out of a rubber band with my tongue?" she said.

Toby started getting a little worried after May had been laughing for five minutes or so. It was only when she calmed down that he noticed that Alice was looking ostentatiously innocent. And Yellowhorse hadn't said another word.

Guys need to stick together sometimes. "So what was the story you have to tell?" he said.

"Right," said Yellowhorse. "Early in the nineteenth century a young writer, living on his wife's inheritance due to his lack of success, was criticizing her taste in reading, asserting that she was damaging her standards of judgment with the novels she bought. Her view was that the books had merit or they could not have attracted a publisher's interest or the public's money. He replied that he was perfectly capable of writing a book that was complete rubbish, but which people would buy because it was exciting to read. She told him to go ahead. He sat down with paper and quill pen and wrote an inflammatory document filled with blood, dramatic speeches, and every error of fact, logic, and consistency he could cram into it. He spent the rest of his life writing sequels. Died fairly rich, and I imagine somewhat bitter. The title of the book was *The Last of the Mohicans*." He waited for any response, got none, and added, "Mark Twain, who had lived for decades on the frontier, went to his grave trying to get people to notice."

After it became apparent that neither of the women had anything to say, Toby said, "I got partway through that in junior high. I believe it."

"I never read it—except the parts Twain quoted," Yellowhorse said. "But I knew the James Fenimore Cooper story. So I set out to write a romance novel with plenty of horses and chocolate in it, and as little sense as I could stomach. Basically as a practical joke. Prison is *boring*. A guy who was getting out after thirty years took the manuscript with him and got it to an agent, and it hit the stands inside of six months. That's very fast for dead-tree publishing. I called it *For the Virgin in Mind*."

"*You're* Narya Farthingsworth?"

It took Toby a moment to realize that both women had said it. He stared at each in turn.

May, at least, had the advantage of having a face that was already much redder than Alice's; but neither would make eye contact.

Yellowhorse had gone on talking. "I split the take three ways: me, my courier, and the woman who showed up for signings. She'd done one porn film, hated it, and had the misfortune of being unforgettable. She got plastic surgery, claimed to be the daughter of a retired Russian mobster and his British mistress, and did a wonderful job. There's an awful lot of really good actresses in porn. Or there were. Haven't checked lately."

"How did you make contact with her?" Toby said.

"Oh, I knew her before I went to work at Littlemeade. You meet the most interesting people at conventions. She did the author picture on all six books, too. Tremendous camera presence, worked great."

"Six?" Toby said.

"*For the Virgin in Mind, Love is a Pineapple, Hallelujah, Bitter Fruit, America's Last Top Model,* and *Where You Find It.* I wrote them like Mad Libs. Use the same plot framework, then plug in nouns, verbs, and adjectives as needed. Losing the family property, tropical island with missionaries, persecuted early Christians, disaffected superhero in jail, post-Apocalypse, and Gold Rush. I squeezed out two a year. Susan got burned out and wanted to retire after number six, and I was glad of the excuse. I was getting cynical even for me."

Toby noticed Alice was wooden-faced. Yellowhorse saw him looking, turned, and said, "Oh dear."

"I *grew up* wanting to be Penny Dreadful," said Alice. "I took martial arts and data analysis."

Yellowhorse was nodding. "*Model* is still the poorest seller. Actually has some literary merit. You'll recall there weren't the usual armadas of motor vehicles. Cars need serious infrastructure, and even in full-on Jonathan Winters smart-ass mode I have my limits. Hence the horses. —After a while, when I saw how the other cons responded to the books, I realized they were potato chips for the soul. Not very nutritious, but something to chew on, and salty. Felt better about taking the money after that."

"They let you have the money in prison?" Alice said.

"Oh, no, my courier set up an investment account for me."

"You trusted him?"

"He was a professional hit man." After a moment he added, "Sorry, you don't know about convicts. As a significant percentage of the U.S. population, they've been developing their own culture. This phenomenon is unique to the United States, because in other countries these are the people who end up working for the government. So: Sexual abusers of any sort are the enemy— most cons have been abused. Molesters tend to have 'accidents' pretty quick, but rapists are mostly just shunned—which in prison is worse than it sounds. Associating only with each other eats away at them. Hit men—as distinct from an ordinary hired killer, who is simply avoided—are so reliable they're sometimes asked to arbitrate disputes. They're in there because they wouldn't rat out their employers. Honorable. Target killers—that is, people who murdered someone and were then done—are often respected but always watched. Since I was a killer who'd targeted a couple of serial rapists, cons treated me about the way freed slaves would treat Lincoln if he showed up. Attentive but not clingy."

Toby thought of something. "Is that where you got the money to get JNAIT set up?"

"Oh, no, it still hasn't come to *that* much. I got most of the seed money from Leslie Reynolds."

Toby gaped. "You know Leslie Reynolds?"

"How do you think I heard about Littlemeade? It's not like you had want ads. I'd run into her husband at a couple of conventions—nicest guy I ever met outside of AA. Good friend of Ivar Jorgenson. You two— Never mind, wandering afield there. Anyway, she ran into me at the freezer vault where his body is. She'd set up a camera to see who was leaving candy. —Lots of people had been leaving flowers, but the concept of killing new life to honor the dead has always bothered me. —His work kept me from killing myself back in the Seventies. We talked, she mentioned Littlemeade, and I thought you might need some ideas. I'm still working on the ice problem."

Toby shook his head. "It's nothing but short progress and dead ends."

"Yeah, but string one idea after another and you get further. It's like dieting. Any diet works for about three weeks, then your progress slows to a crawl. What you do, you go on a new diet every three weeks."

"That's ridiculous," said Toby.

"It works," said Alice. "I lost sixty pounds in a year that way. Kept it off. Got my comfort-eating under control. It's what Sylvia Noonan did in *Bitter Fruit*."

The Rukh beneath them turned and started accelerating up the runway. May heard and felt the roar in her bones and was satisfied: it was as she had imagined. Her passengers sagged back in their seats, stopped trying to talk and simply experienced.

When they were in the air, the sound became a whistling hush. Alice wondered, "Mycroft, how did you get the tribes to adopt you? It had to be before they were taking immigrants, and they couldn't know about the bots yet."

"They didn't. It involved drugs and explosive casting. I do have some American ancestry, judging by facial bones . . . and an interestingly mysterious smile I saw on an old picture of my great-grandmother. . . . Most likely from somewhere in the Rockies. It isn't a big enough percentage to claim tribal status, though. Having *some* Indian blood in the U.S. is about as rare as finding a successful bar next to a medical school. What I did, I found some people who were just trying to mind their own business and live their lives, and showed them how to stop being bothered by patronizing anthropologists. Any tribesman who isn't willing to play a practical joke on Europeans is obviously some kind of mole for Indian Affairs, so it went great. They'd pick the leader of some 'expedition'—defined as a professor and several assistants who wanted to go camping on somebody's rangeland—hint about a secret ceremony, and allow themselves to be bribed into letting him see it. Then they'd make him fast for three days, stuff him full of peyote, and take him into the inner sanctum where the holy of holies was kept. This would turn out to be a steel plate that had been deformed into the shape of the front half of a coyote."

There was a silence that seemed much longer than it

was. They could hear the liquid oxygen start pumping into *Firebird*'s tank.

"What?" said Alice.

"None of them ever came back," Mycroft added.

"They really did it?" May said.

"Repeatedly. In several places. Nobody ever came back. Or talked about it. I've been waiting to hear something, but I don't expect to. Anthropologists do get some silly notions, like 'people so primitive they don't know what causes pregnancy'—hell, *cats* know what causes pregnancy! Why else does a tomcat get the crap beat out of him after he's done?—but this would be like going to a meeting of UFOlogists, and saying you were taken aboard a flying saucer and met Santa Claus."

Toby suddenly said, "Ha! Maybe the aliens have figured that out, so that's what they do to the people who are *really* abducted." He grinned disturbingly.

"Toby," said Mycroft, "if there were genuine aliens watching us, and they wanted to be ignored, all they had to do from Day One was paint WHAM-O on the side of the ship. —And why would they care if we're getting enough fiber?"

"Mycroft," said May, laughing, "never make the pilot unable to concentrate."

"Tell Toby. I'm not even in arm's reach."

"Help me out here, Alice," May said. "Stuff something in his mouth if you have to."

Silence.

They looked at Alice. She looked away, out the tiny elliptical window. After a bit she said, "I never get the references."

Toby said, "It has been getting a bit—"

"Moslem. We read the Koran. No, I never got as far as Terry Pratchett. The jokes just keep whizzing past my head. Sorry."

"I can stop," Mycroft said. "I should have been paying attention, Alice. I was trying to distract myself."

Toby said, "From what?"

"This," Mycroft said, and the motors went off. They were falling free. Then something clunked beneath them, and something whooshed, and they sagged back in their seats as the Rukh began using its oxygen and became a rocket.

Toby said, "We watched you touch down on target during a skydiving contest."

"You're falling for a few seconds. Your whole body thinks you've been murdered. Then the air buoys you up and you're flying. This is going to be different. In twelve minutes May will turn off the rocket and we'll *fall*. Falling is one of the only ways nobody ever tried to kill me. Got no tolerance."

"All right," Alice said soothingly. "Tell a joke. Then explain it."

XXVIII

Always listen to experts. They'll tell you what can't be done, and why. Then do it.

—ROBERT ANSON HEINLEIN

Jack Bernstein had mixed feelings about being NASA's token Jewish astronaut.

His technical knowledge and mechanical ability were the best in the astronaut corps, but he didn't have the reflexes of some of the candidates who were passed over. He had to admit it wasn't fair.

Weighing heavily against that was the fact that the current administration's Middle East policy was one of pressuring Israel into policies that would, if enacted, destroy it as a nation. The official position was that this was motivated by compassion, and not because Bob Foster belonged to a Party whose leaders had been openly indifferent to the mass murder of Jews for more than a century—barring one exception, and he died young.

The clincher was, if they wanted to maintain the pose, they *had* to send him into space.

Screw fair.

* * *

He showed up late at the ready room. "Bernstein!" snapped General Quinn. "Where the hell have you been?"

"Ordering breakfast, sir," he said.

"We've got breakfast waiting on *you*!"

"This is an *astronaut's* breakfast, sir," Jack said, and held open the door for the catering crew.

The first platter was set before Sam Quinn and uncovered as Jack sat down.

The Healthy Balanced Appropriate Meal that NASA had been inflicting on crews for years looked pitiful at the best of times, but next to the rare rib-eye steak and poached eggs—hot out of the kitchen in the truck—it looked downright contemptible.

Quinn was biting his lip, trying not to smile.

None of the other three were trying at all.

Stephen Edmundson wasn't trying because he wasn't happy. "This is contrary to nutritional policy," he said.

Martin Tillery, next to him, obligingly took Edmundson's platter, cut the steak into four pieces, and divided it, the eggs, and the fried potatoes among the other four plates without a word.

Charley Loomis, mouth full, nodded at Tillery, then beamed at Jack. Then he swallowed some of what he had in his mouth to make room for more.

Edmundson ate his oatmeal and raw vegetables with icy dignity.

By and by Quinn mopped his mouth, hove a great sigh, and said, "Men, the mission plan has been updated. A flight commissioned by the Joint Negotiating Alliance of Indian Tribes has been launched from Ecuador, and it's believed that it'll attempt to take control of the nanomachines that are controlling the asteroid. An attempt to block it failed, and the JNAIT mission was sent up early, so they're not in the window for fast rendezvous, but there's a good chance they'll arrive while we're there. We have to prevent our opposition from reaching the nanomachines, because if they do JNAIT will be in a position to hold the entire world for ransom. Our cargo has been accordingly modified. —In the course of this mission, we will be maintaining radio silence whenever possible. There is reason to believe the opposition has excellent counterintelligence."

To wit, guns. Great. War goes to space. Jack held his tongue, but he could see that Tillery and Loomis were as dismayed as he was.

Edmundson, of course, was delighted. "What are our options, General?" he said.

"Orders from the president are to do whatever is necessary." Quinn frowned. "My orders to you are to do *only* what's necessary. So far the United States of America has never engaged any country in a war of aggression, and we're not starting one on my watch."

"General, the Tribes aren't a country. They've never been recognized by the U.S., sir," Edmundson said.

"They've been recognized by China and India, Major, both of whom would be very happy for a pretext to cut off trade with us. Most American industries are dependent on those countries to function. If you have a problem with this mission, perhaps if we're lucky we can find someone else in the next sixty minutes."

The standby list for any given mission was pretty much every member of the corps. The only one not on it today, if Jack recalled, was Doug Waterhouse, who was having some kind of intensive dental surgery—and chances were, *he'd* be willing to take some Demerol and tie his jaw shut.

Edmundson, however, had gotten his job because the Senate majority leader owed a media trillionaire a lot of favors. "So do we just wait for them to shoot first, or until they actually hit someone?" he said. "Sir."

Quinn gave him the look he might have given a bug in the soup. "Are you certain you're *appropriately motivated,* Major?"

The managerial buzzword got through where sarcasm hadn't. "Oh, yes, sir!"

"Very well. I will assess the situation as it develops, and direct our response. —Apart from that, we proceed as planned: find and disable the main computer of the Briareus mission."

A little before Jack had been accepted as an astronaut, NASA had grudgingly switched over to spacesuits that hadn't been designed by dead Germans. Since he was the youngest man in the present crew, that meant he got to hear bitter reminiscences about the old gear while they were all dressing. He nodded and agreed with everyone; as a tech guy, his own irritation was focused on the fact that they were about to be taken into space by a system the United States could have used a year after the Blackbird was built.

And calling it "subcontracting" didn't change the fact

that they'd had to buy it from an outfit NASA had driven out of the country.

He continued to hold his tongue while they checked each other's suits and plugged their own into their support packs. The new suits also had backpacks you could swing off and get at in a timely fashion, i.e., before you died.

When the van dropped them off at their ride, he was the last man out.

Each man before him had stopped dead for a moment, even Edmundson. So did Jack. He'd seen pictures of a Rukh, but the reality was beyond any photo or even video. Aside from being NASA white, it looked like a Blackbird had had a heavy date with a Valkyrie, which latter had subsequently mainlined growth hormones during gestation, then fed the offspring red meat from birth. The piggybacked *orbiter* was big enough to carry a Shuttle. Either Shuttle.

The orbiter had a couple of solid cores strapped to its fuselage. Granted, they were in a race; but another word for monopropellant, as Richard Feynman had pointed out, was "explosive."

And some NASA penny saver in an office in D.C. had arranged for a ladder, for five men, in spacesuits, to climb, to board an orbiter that was being sent in such a hurry that it had slowly-detonating bombs attached.

Fortunately the firemen in the ground crew had glommed a couple of cherrypickers, and they were all aboard in a few minutes. On his way up, Jack glanced at the port window of the Rukh cockpit, and saw a couple of well-formed pink cheeks pressed against the glass. One had an odd mark. He swung down the Fresnel visor, and was just able to make out a tattoo of a hornet. He'd seen it before, at the beach.

He'd just edged out Claire Daughenbaugh in qualifying for this mission. Her present commentary on being part of the lifter crew could be construed as a mixed message, possibly worth clarifying later. "Did anyone else notice Daughenbaugh on the way up?" he said as he closed the door behind him.

"Yeah, she waved at us too," said Loomis.

Almost certainly worth clarifying later.

XXIX

Ye may kill for yourselves and your mates
And your cubs as they need, and ye can,
But kill not for pleasure of killing,
And seven times never kill Man!

—RUDYARD KIPLING

The Rukh was pulling up from its acceleration dive. To get to launch altitude, which was too high for even hypersonic ramjets to breathe, and to get back down to cruising level, it was now using the LOX it had made but hadn't pumped into the *Firebird*. A Rukh had a considerably better glide ratio than anything designed by a committee of politicians, but deadstick flight was for kamikazes.

The sound of air along the fuselage gradually faded to nothing.

It suddenly struck Toby: "You know, this is the craziest thing I've done in my life."

Yellowhorse spoke up for the first time in a while. "Oh, I don't know. What about running naked over the hood of a police cruiser and making a getaway through a biker bar?"

The seats would still swivel as long as the engine wasn't lit. He turned to stare at Yellowhorse, and became aware as he did so that both women were staring at *him*. "I never did any such thing!"

Yellowhorse gave him a blank look. Then he looked sharply at May, gave Toby a look of comprehension, and looked at May again. "Right. —I'm thinking of someone else," he told May firmly. He followed this with a glance toward Toby, and a microscopic nod.

As the torch lit and his seat automatically swung to face forward again, Toby was inarticulate.

No comment from May; despite what she'd said, when she was being a pilot, she was all business.

Alice, on the other hand, displayed a remarkable ability to laugh extensively under high thrust.

God*damn,* this bird was hot! May leveled off the *Firebird* at a million feet. They'd have to wait most of an orbit for the next burn to get them to the . . . huh, it wasn't really a rock anymore, was it?

Come to think of it, what they were heading toward was First Contact with an alien spacecraft. Nanomachines were a nonhuman intelligence, and the ones that were up there had decidedly not been "born" on Earth.

Make that just plain born, no quotation marks. They were alive by any definition that made sense to May.

"Yellowhorse," she said, "you may be the biggest smart-ass I've ever even heard of, but you sure know how to build a rocket."

"Praise from Caesar is praise indeed," he said.

"*Firebird,* this is Cosmos," she heard. "We have sighted another launch vehicle headed toward the Equator. Origin Cape Canaveral," said PdC Traffic Control. "It handles as if it is much heavier than your flight. We have options. Over."

"Roger that, Cosmos. —NASA's got their bird up, and the cargo bay's full," she told the others, primarily Yellowhorse. "Both Ground and I doubt it's beads and blankets. Ground can shoot 'em down if we want."

"*We don't,*" Yellowhorse said immediately. "A human who knowingly starts a space war dies memorably. Trust me on this."

"Cosmos, this is *Firebird*. Leave 'em alone, we're good. —*How* memorably?"

"You know what a test pilot looks like after a bad mistake?"

"Jesus," said May.

"More like Joan of Arc, actually. —Anyhow, this is worse. Briefly. On the bright side, there's not much to clean up."

"How the hell can nanos do that?" Toby said.

"I'm not going to tell you."

"He's not," Alice said.

"I know," Toby said. "He's said that to me before."

"Oh, of course."

"I just can't imagine how nanos could do something like that. —I refuse to *believe* you've got them set up for fusion."

The sound and thrust of the *Firebird*'s rocket sagged to nothing. They were falling.

Everyone was looking at Yellowhorse.

"You have time to paint each other's suits now," Yellowhorse said.

"We are *not* opening paint containers in free fall," May said. "Not on my watch."

"Dang. You're right. I should have put it into markers," said Yellowhorse.

"How would that be fun?" Alice said.

May saw Toby shake his head once, sharply. She grinned as he said, "Right. —Mycroft, how did you get your nanos into Wade Curtis?"

"BB gun," said Yellowhorse. "Quit staring at me. I've been murdered. It was a lot worse than this."

"You *shot* him?"

"I was pressed for time. He's not a man who accepts things without hard evidence, even if he likes the premise, and I needed to hurry so I could get myself arrested. I wanted to do that before those monsters killed again. All things considered, I think he'll forgive me . . . assuming he hasn't figured it out already. He's awfully smart. —With Leslie Reynolds, now, I just explained things and gave her a trace of blood in some soup, same as the convicts later. She just got the virus-eater and network back then. Not as advanced as what the convicts got, but she was hardly about to go tormenting people. She's got the upgrade now, like you. Bacterial breakdown, gene repair, cell reconstruction, vitamin synthesis, mineral reclamation, the works. Handshake. She's still got some waiting to do." He sounded gloomy.

"What happens to old bots when the new ones show up?" Toby said.

"They're ignored, unless you've got the upgrade. Then they're stripped for parts."

"And the network can recognize the act of starting a war?" Toby said, sounding alarmed.

"It can. Relax, doing something that forces someone else to act is a more basic concept than you realize."

"Bullying," said May.

Toby spoke slowly: "Isn't that what a baby does when he cries?"

"I should have said 'deliberately,'" Yellowhorse said. "No doubt there are babies who do it when they're just bored, to see the commotion, but nowadays I reckon those'll get tired of it pretty quick. Most cry because they're genuinely unhappy about something. Toby, relax, I mean it. The network in your body has enormous scope but very little depth. Three connectors per bot."

"That's it?"

"I wanted to improve humanity, not replace it."

XXX

For another, better thing than a fight required of duty
Exists not for a warrior.

—THE BHAGAVAD GITA

1

The inhabitants of Foundry watched with interest as two spaceplanes began working their way outward to meet them. Both were similar to a design they had expected, but neither matched it exactly. One handled clumsily, but had boosters attached. The other had a hotter drive, but aside from that was unarmed.

When it became clear that the one with weapons aboard was trying to catch the unarmed one, there was some discussion of what to do. It would take a while for the leading ship to be caught. There was time to decide.

2

Sam Quinn hailed the JNAIT ship as soon as it was clear they were going to be able to catch it. "Attention unidentified craft. This is the NASA spaceplane *Envoy*. You appear to be shaping course toward the property of the United States. You will desist and stand by for further instructions. Over."

A woman's voice replied. "Good morning, *Envoy*. As you are perfectly aware, this is the Joint Negotiating Alliance of Indian Tribes vessel *Firebird*, and what we are approaching is private property. The U.S. is signatory to several treaties which establish, among other things, that eminent domain does not extend beyond the atmosphere. They also establish that we are in international territory. Therefore any attempt to interfere with us will be regarded as piracy. And not just by JNAIT. —Incidentally, you are in a spaceship which I designed. You might at least make an effort to fly the thing right. *Firebird* out."

Edmundson spoke up. "Shall I check the cargo, General?"

"No. Commander Tillery, you and Dr. Bernstein do that. Commodore Loomis and Major Edmundson, carry on as before." He switched over his mike and began talking with the Cape. Stephen frowned over his monitor, Charley smiled over his, and Jack and Marty unstrapped and went aft down the ladders on the ceiling.

The lock between cabin and cargo was big enough for both of them, and since the cargo bay had already had its air removed, their suit heaters switched on as the air in the lock was condensed out. Less power than a NASA lock, and it saved more atmosphere. Also faster, so Jack didn't have time to brood over it.

The cargo was more than enough to brood over.

After they'd gotten down to the aft bulkhead and done an overview of the larger boxes, Marty said, "Well, at least there isn't a nuke."

"Yeah, Bob Foster's not stupid enough to repeat what happened to China," Jack replied, opening a smaller crate. "Not quite."

"Hey, that's my commander in chief you're talking about," Marty said.

"What do you want, pity?"

"Nah, save that for when the monster jumps out and gets us."

"Huh?"

"You know. The minority characters die heroically and the WASPs save the day. Don't you watch movies?"

Jack snorted. "More than I ever wanted. —And it's the black guy that gets to die heroically. The Jew is the one who antagonizes the monster in the first place, when it just wanted peaceful coexistence."

Marty shrugged. "For that matter, Steve's a Social Humanist."

"Right, I forgot. That makes *him* the hero. Sacrificing himself for the sake of humanity."

"To nanomachines? I don't see him allowing something to take over his brain."

"Wouldn't be the first time." Jack looked unhappily at the target-seeker he'd just revealed. "All this shit is for use on human beings," he said.

"Oh, get serious. *All* weapons are for use on human beings," Marty said. "What did you expect, little teeny bullets? It's reasonable that the nanomachines would armor the computer. It's their brain, it needs a skull. This stuff is to punch through it."

"*This* warhead is shrapnel. You're Navy. Is there some point in attacking a battleship with shotguns? Shaped-charge shells would make sense. Twenty consecutive shaped charges would drill into Cheyenne Mountain, and leave room in this hold for a brass band. Instead—" He gestured at the crates. "She's right, we've been sent up here to be pirates."

Marty shook his head. "Quinn wouldn't do it."

"Edmundson would."

"So we watch him."

"And what, shoot him?" Jack turned to look at Marty.

Marty looked thoughtful. "Well . . . maybe not. I was raised to avoid self-indulgence. —There should be something nonlethal amongst all this. Pirates do take hostages and hold them for ransom."

They went on looking. After a while Jack chuckled and said, "If this were a movie you'd be a Moslem."

"If this were a movie, you'd be Daughenbaugh, and we'd be back here making out. Focus on the job, will you? I'm in a bad enough mood without getting depressed too."

XXXI

God does not play dice with the Universe.

—ALBERT EINSTEIN

Stop telling God what to do!

—NIELS BOHR

Time had been passing, conversation had wandered, and Mycroft had been holding forth.

He did that.

"——What they overlook is that relativity is a model. It's a really *good* model, but a time machine that uses relativity theory to work is a Hieronymus device."

"Whisky Tango Foxtrot?" said Alice.

"Sorry. It's something that attempts to affect reality by manipulating symbols."

"Like the Federal Reserve?" she said.

She sounded like she might be kidding, but Mycroft said, "Don't do that, it's spooky. That's the example I was about to use. —The trouble is, nobody nowadays is in a position to notice, because nobody's done any physics since 1987. A supernova was seen then, fifty thousand parsecs away, and the neutrino pulse arrived before the light, but the Global Warming cult insisted on the three-neutrino hypothesis getting all the grant money, and for that to be right, neutrinos have to have mass."

Alice objected, "But nobody believes in Global Warming now."

"Your phrasing implies that they believed in it *then*. Check the records. Everyone who claimed to be concerned about it was involved in causes with an agenda of increasing control over private life. They took over basic research, and their political heirs still control it. —Matter of fact, Wade Curtis had already done a disturbingly good story series about politicians taking over the world that way."

Toby had read most of it. "Disturbingly good" said it pretty well. He had experience getting William Connors back on track: "So, assuming some kind of time machine you can use without leaving Earth, what's your target?"

"Zurich, 1916," Mycroft said at once. "Frame Lenin for bank robbery. He never gets out, the Russian Army doesn't have its supply lines sabotaged, Kerensky's Republic isn't overthrown and doesn't surrender, the War is prosecuted until Germany is crushed, Wilson is dead of another stroke by then and can't taint the treaty, the German Empire is broken back up into multiple states, von Ludendorff goes off to write ponderous memoirs and never founds the National Socialists, Adolf Hitler ends up in used cars or real estate or something that makes use of his one talent, the German banking system is never unified enough to collapse in 1927, the Bubble of 1929 isn't as severe and leaves the U.S. better off than the rest of the world, Charles Curtis is elected in 1932 and cuts taxes, the physicists of Europe come to the U.S. and the first reactor is built around 1936, no Holocaust, no Cold War, and no free guns given to millions of maniacs in the Middle East because nobody needs the oil that bad. Mind you, China would Balkanize after Sun-Yat-Sen's dictatorship failed for lack of Russian support, and the neofeudalists in Japan would be grabbing off chunks, which would lead to war between Japan and England, but I think I could deal with that as it arose. I wouldn't remake Goat Flu until Wilson was dead. You?"

He'd clearly been thinking about it for some time. At a huge disadvantage, and wishing he hadn't suggested the game, Toby said, "Woodstock."

"Oh, good one! Smooch a lot of girls, spread the bots through the leftist population, and Congress never sabotages the space program because anyone who proposes it drops dead of a stroke. I like it. Who goes next?"

"Cut off John Wilkes Booth's big toes so he can't climb a flight of stairs," said May.

"Huh!" said Mycroft. "In the Minimalist event we might just have a gold. Unless you've got one, Alice?"

"Go back to be your girlfriend in high school," she said. "I'd just like to see what you'd have done if you were healthy."

"I'm declaring a winner," said Toby.

May said, "We'll reach the rock in an hour and ten minutes. Brake first, of course."

Toby asked, "How are you doing, Mycroft?"

"Fine. You? Alice? You never know until you're there."

"Good," said Alice, and Toby said, "I was born falling." They fell.

Mycroft said, "I got through customs once by asking

the guy how many people a year thought they were making an original joke, and didn't know the difference between 'declare' and 'declaim.' He just laughed and waved me past."

"What was in your luggage?" Toby said.

"Underwear."

"Well, don't go making it sound like you pulled a fast one," Toby said.

"It was his wife's."

All three listeners said, "*What?*"

"Okay, I made that part up. —I just didn't want the hassle."

Alice began laughing helplessly. May said, "He's like this all the time, isn't he?"

"Pretty much. I'd hate to tell you what happened at my aunt's funeral," said Toby.

"Hey!" Mycroft said, indignant. Then he laughed. "Okay, you got me."

"Stop, I can't wipe my eyes in this thing," Alice said, still laughing.

"Screen on the left forearm," Mycroft said. "Scroll down to blue, zoom the face, and fingermouse. Red is scratching. Green is blowing your nose."

May gaped at him, then looked at Alice. "My God. Even Heinlein didn't think of that one."

"I wouldn't care to bet," Mycroft said. "All we know is he didn't put it in a story. And it might have been in an unmutilated version of *Have Spacesuit—Will Travel*."

"I could just beat the crap out of that editor he had, when I think what's been lost," Alice said. When they all looked at her, she said, "I may not be a diehard sci-fi fan, but I'm not illiterate."

"She's long dead," Mycroft told her. "The dogs'll get her."

"Dogs?"

"In Hell, people who destroy treasure for a feeling of power are put in a bleak forest where they're chased and torn apart by dogs," Mycroft said. "Dante Alighieri."

"Lot of mothers there," she said.

"He didn't say."

"I wasn't asking."

"I wasn't arguing."

Toby's mother had been a warm, gentle woman, whose one vice was grafting new slips onto what had ultimately become an extremely strange-looking apple tree, and he *really* didn't want to hear any more on this topic. He supposed his reaction was akin to survivor's guilt, but he still changed the subject. "You got an attachment for gum on these suits?" he said.

"Damn," Mycroft said. "Let me make a note for the next model." They were all silent for a while. Then Mycroft said, "Done."

"You're actually doing it?"

"Gum is very comforting. Great idea."

"Uh-oh. They're matching course with us. Crap," May said. Then she swung her arm around without looking, to point unerringly at Mycroft. "Say it and I hit your ejector switch."

"There'd be no *point* saying it *now*," Mycroft said, sounding huffy.

"I'm not used to being the dumbest one in the room," said Alice. "Say what?"

"'Have some gum,' or words to that effect," May said. "This man is always On."

"Not really. He prefers under."

Even if Toby cut his microphone and opaqued his helmet, May would have seen him shaking. He held it in.

"*Et tu*, Alice?" said May.

"Actually—"

"Let it go," said Mycroft.

Toby still held it in. It occurred to him that after this exercise of will, levitation might be worth a try.

"They're still about ten miles away," May said. "Close enough to have shot us with something by now, so I'd say that confirms they want Toby alive."

XXXII

Oaths are but words, and words but wind.

—*SAMUEL BUTLER*

1

"As I see it, our best course is to take control of the other craft and dump LOX until they have just enough to get home," said Sam.

"General, have you considered taking the crew aboard as prisoners and having one of us fly it back?" said Stephen.

"Why not just make them walk the plank?" said Jack.

"I was making a suggestion. Do you have to be so nosy?" Stephen said.

"You forgot to say 'you people,'" said Marty.

"I have had about enough of you reading things into what I say."

"You forgot to say 'you people,'" said Marty.

"*Listen—*"

Sam cut everyone's mikes. "Now hear this," he said in a voice gone dangerously quiet. "When we have matched course, we will grapple, close, and take control of the other craft. We are here to prevent the world from being taken prisoner. In the course of this, we are obliged to set an example of lawful behavior. If anyone has any doubts about what constitutes lawful behavior, say so and you will be relieved of duty. Are there any questions?" He turned the mikes back on.

Edmundson kept his mouth shut. Jack wished he had his cell camera. There were astronauts who would pay to see that.

2

Foundry's surface was pretty well covered with a phase-coordinated telescope array, much less vulnerable than a single mirror, vastly larger in aperture, and far easier to aim. Set had been disturbed by the exchange of radio messages earlier, and was now even more disturbed by the deliberation of the second ship's approach. The concept of bluffing was known from monitoring broadcasts—a job that grew constantly bigger as they got closer to Earth—but the examples of how stupid it was to assume someone was doing so were numerous, and most of them were not fiction.

The messages they had had to decode from military "encryption"—as the senders considered it—had always been disturbing, but they were getting worse.

More disturbing yet was the fact that, if the ships maintained their courses, rendezvous would occur while they were on the other side of the Earth from Foundry. It was as if the pursuers had planned that.

Set passed on his concerns to the rest. Shortly after

the message had been sent to Forge, a reply came from Socrates:

Send your own intercept craft.

A design suggestion followed almost ten seconds later; clearly it had been given a lot of thought. It was simple and could be made from parts on hand.

It was launched in twenty minutes.

XXXIII

*[He] had heard of fighting fair, and had long ago
decided he wanted no part of it.*

—TERRY PRATCHETT

1

As *Envoy* was closing with *Firebird,* Mycroft said, "I can hit their windshield from here."

The U.S. ship was about a quarter of a mile away. "With what, your new nanos?" said May.

"Some of them, certainly, but most would just end up adrift, and I'd rather not. I was thinking of using one of the guns Alice was thoughtful enough to collect while I was doing first aid. They'd have to rely on us to get them home."

May turned to look at each of them in turn, then settled on Mycroft. "I didn't see her do that."

"Neither did I, but her bag was about sixty pounds heavier than it had been. Not every kind of intelligence shows up on an IQ test."

"Huh," said May, as Alice looked pleased. "Wouldn't that be an act of war?"

"They're not asking permission to come alongside," Mycroft said. "And their cargo bay is opening. QED, they are engaged in piracy."

May turned swiftly and checked her screen. He was right. Four astronauts were visible coming out of the cargo bay, and they were all carrying equipment. She narrowed her eyes. "That's all right," she said. "I've got this." She tapped her keyboard and sent a message to the other ship's BIOS.

The reentry shield on *Envoy*'s belly detached and began moving away from the spaceplane.

When May turned to look at Mycroft again, he was watching his own screen in silence, his mouth hanging open. "You're not the only one who prepares for emergencies," she said. She switched to voice transmission and hailed the other ship.

2

Charles Stuart Loomis had always had a curious advantage over most members of the astronaut corps: he never showed any trace of bone loss no matter how much time he spent in free fall. He'd also spent five of the past six years concealing a severe and progressive combination of rheumatoid and osteoarthritis—the same trouble that had driven his mother to suicide. Early in '51 he began suspecting a decline in mental clarity as well. While pain wouldn't stop him from doing a good job, hiding a lack of alertness would have been criminal, so he'd started giving himself regular intelligence tests. The results had been equivocal . . . until he took an IQ test the day after Thanksgiving, and scored thirty points higher than he had two weeks before. Five days later, he'd been about to take his morning ketoprofen and suddenly realized the redness, pain, and swelling in his knuckles were gone.

He was also having no more trouble keeping his weight down—everything he ate wasn't automatically put into storage. His wife Jennifer thought it might be due to her renewed interest in him . . . or his increased energy may have been the cause of that interest. Or both. In any case, it was like being kids again; if they had an important appointment somewhere, they didn't dare change clothes in the same room.

Charley thought it had something to do with nobody getting AIDS anymore.

When he learned about the mission, to rendezvous with what had been the target of a nanotech probe, he'd realized immediately that Toby Glyer would be trying to get there any way he could too; and Charley Loomis resolved not to let anything bad happen to Toby Glyer.

In the course of twenty years in the astronaut corps, he had overheard what turned out, when he thought about it, to be a staggering amount of dirt on any number of influential people in the NASA and Navy hierarchies— all of which he now recalled with a clarity that still amazed him. He'd gone to have a few little chats with some of them, and had ended up being the first man chosen for the *Envoy* mission. He'd also been promoted from captain to commodore, a rank typically used only in wartime. As a flag officer, he'd have been mission commander, if not for the fact that President Foster was an Air Force fighter jockey. Still, for someone who was a pilot rather than an aviator, Brigadier General Samson Quinn was steady enough.

Unfortunately, that meant that Charley, as second in command, had to wait in the truck.

Of course, in the present circumstances, perhaps that wasn't unfortunate. The other four had all gone back to the hold to gird up their loins or whatever, and Charley sat watching the instruments.

There was a little bump.

The heat shield light went red.

He tapped keys at high speed. It had jettisoned. "Jesus H. FUCK!" he yelled, and hit the command link. "General, our reentry shield has just separated, and the computer says it was our idea. I wasn't touching the board. I think it's an override command."

"Good day, gentlemen," the woman piloting the other ship said into all their earphones. "I am certain you will be relieved to learn that you are still able to land without burning up. It requires only that you turn your ship, burn just about all your fuel coming to a halt relative to the ground, and fly your craft down as an airplane. Of course, you only have enough fuel to do that with an empty cargo bay. I suggest you dump it out now."

"That's the first shot," Sam said.

Stephen had a recoilless, and he started to put a rocket into it.

Jack and Marty had chosen adhesive-restraint launchers, whose ammo was popularly known as "booger bombs." Two of them hit Stephen just about simultaneously, and began foaming up and forcing his arms away from his torso. "What is *wrong* with you two?" he demanded.

"Don't know about Marty," said Jack, "but with me it's that whole 'thou shalt not kill' thing."

"Works for me," said Marty.

"Take him back in," said Sam, taking the launcher.

The two of them each had one hand on Stephen and one hand on their lines when Sam locked on and put a shaped-charge target-seeker through *Firebird*'s LOX tank.

"Jesus, Sam!" said Jack.

"I have very clear orders from the president," said Sam, not sounding like he objected to them.

Then his helmet burst.

They got him into a survival bubble, because that's what you do, but Jack didn't expect much. Sam's head was charred, and his body was hot enough to feel through Jack's gloves. He could feel brittle crackles as they bent Sam's arms enough to get him into the bubble.

Something caught his eye, and he looked up to see a thing like two fat metal donuts on a meshwork pipe come apart between the ships. One of the donuts shot itself along the pipe and disappeared ahead of them. The other one, still on the pipe, took up station above the open hold, and pointed a lot of thin rods at *Envoy*.

Jack was keenly reminded of why this mission was so important. *Firebird* was not the threat.

XXXIV

Go to the ant, thou sluggard; consider her ways,
and be wise.

—PROVERBS

1

"Looks like our ride's here," said Mycroft over the radio
as he headed for the cargo lock. The rest were staring in
horror at their screens. "Good, NASA will assume the
bots had something to do with it. — Spontaneous human
combustion," he added. "Or, in the words of Alex Cox,
'People just explode.' I once worked out that if all the
potassium-40 in the human body decayed at once, it
would reduce the carbon in the tissues with superheated
steam, and the hydrogen that was produced would be hot
enough to ignite spontaneously. In a pressure suit the fire
is confined to your head and lungs. The bots are perfectly capable of aligning atoms so their nuclei are or-
thogonal to solar neutrinos, which are likewise perfectly
capable of inducing decay. I have no idea how it happens
naturally. Never been able to reproduce any psychic phenomena under controlled conditions, so—"

"Will you *shut* UP?" Toby half screamed.

Mycroft grunted. Then Toby heard him say, "Got
your first job for you, ladies. —Can somebody else get

back here and hold the other light? The hole is all the way through."

"I'll do it," Toby muttered, and unstrapped to follow Mycroft.

It wasn't as easy as Mycroft had made it look. By the time Toby reached the access hatch at the rear of the cargo bay, sweat was soaking through the fabric of his suit. As soon as he opened it, however, his heaters switched on.

Mycroft was shining searing violet light down one side of the tank. There was oxygen frosted against most of the surfaces Toby could see, except where the light shone directly. "Got the other light? I can't turn right now."

"Yeah," Toby said, and went to the darker side of the tank. He could see where LOX was boiling out of the hole, freezing as its pressure dropped. "You got some more nanos?"

"They're all over the tank."

"Okay." He switched on the light he'd picked up in the bay, and started getting warmer at once. He aimed it at the leak.

In all these years, he'd never gotten to watch nanos at work.

At first, he still didn't. The glare of his light was too dazzling. After a minute or so his eyes had adjusted enough to see that there was a black splotch flowing into the hole, and that the spray was slowing. He adjusted his aim. "You brought in more metal?" he said.

"Ruthenium steel, twelve percent," Mycroft said. "I had it in my bag, for just such occasions. They've got it."

"Pricey."

"Not for much longer. —I've got the exit hole here. Your side should be closing up sooner, so when it does, bring the light over. Slow, so they follow."

"Right." They were silent for a while, then Toby said, "I don't see any more fog. I'll give them time to finish up here."

"No, they can do the outer shell when the leak's stopped here. Come *now*."

Toby moused the black patch over to the other side, then said, "Holy crap, dude."

"Yeah. Says something about May's taste in tank liners that we've got any oxygen left at all. Lost about a third, I'd guess." The hole in the outer shell of the LOX tank was big enough for May to have slipped through without scratching her tanks. Oxygen was still coming out the inner shell, but it slowed visibly as the second splotch arrived.

"Do we have enough to get home?" Toby said.

"Not an issue. Even if the bots on the Rock haven't hung on to any oxygen, I hardly think May's going to let *Envoy* go anywhere. And they've got plenty."

When the venting stopped, the big splotch moved outward and began closing the outer shell of the tank. "Now you can move them back," Mycroft said. "Sunlight should be enough for them to handle the hull. May can roll the ship."

"Mycroft, I'm sorry I flipped out like that."

"Why?"

"Hell, the man's *head* exploded!"

"I know. I meant, 'Why are you sorry?' It was the most

shocking and inexplicable thing I could come up with. I *want* people to flip out when someone pulls that crap. You'll notice they haven't tried anything else."

"At the moment it's not them I'm worried about," Toby said. "The Briareus nanos still aren't talking to us, remember?"

Mycroft gave him a funny look, but said only, "I'll stay here and collect these after."

"Mycroft," Alice's voice said, "I've been thinking."

"Hardly unusual," he said. "Interesting subject, I take it?"

"The jihad threat. That's a bluff."

"Hell it is. Bots separate isotopes just fine."

"Yes, but all the people who are willing to send credulous idiots out as human bombs are dead by now, aren't they?"

After a moment Mycroft's breathing could be heard again. Then he said, "I am hampered in expressing myself by the lack of a sufficiently vehement expletive in the English language. I never thought of that. Alice?"

"Yes?"

"Don't you dare call yourself dumb in my hearing again."

2

After they'd been chucking the armaments out of the cargo bay for a few minutes, Stephen said, "Spray me off, I'll help."

Jack found some solvent and turned him loose.

"That would have been me," Stephen said once he got a look at Sam.

They closed the bay and left Sam there, moored to a bulkhead. There was plenty of room.

Envoy's cargo bay air lock readout had a melted screen. So did all their suits' wrist monitors. Their radios still worked, and Charley cycled the lock for them.

The cockpit screens were okay. Whatever they'd been hit with was localized.

"Helm doesn't respond," said Charley. "I think we may have to rely on charity for a ride home."

"Might be worth asking, Commodore," said Stephen. "They don't want us dead."

"How do you know?"

"We're not dead."

Jack took a long look at him. This did not sound like the Stephen Edmundson he knew. Come to think of it, that one would have been ranting and assigning blame from the moment Sam Quinn blew up.

Evidently it wasn't the one Charley Loomis knew either. "When did you get all calm and analytical?"

"When two guys I never got along with saved my life by accident. And didn't say a thing about it. Not even that they should have let me go ahead and do the shooting. That's kind of hard not to think about. After a while it seemed to me that there were other things I should be thinking about too."

"The hole's closing up," said Marty. They all checked their screens. *Firebird* was looking pretty good.

Stephen said, "That thing out there could have sprayed nanomachines at them, or they might have brought some along. Or, hell, they could be built in. I think that could be a popular idea after this."

"NASA's administration won't like it," said Jack. "Gray goo scenario."

"The Holy Roman Emperor might not like it because it gives the peasant class too much leisure time," Charley said. "There still is an heir, you know. Saw a news item. He makes model animals. Glassblowing. The idea of NASA having any authority left at this point seems like a pretty weak joke."

"Hello again," said *Firebird*'s pilot. "The way I see it, you owe us some LOX."

Charley said, "We didn't bring a pipe."

"We should have one by the time you get here. You'll

need a ride after that. You want to come along, or shall we come back for you?"

"We're not that attached to this ship," Charley said. "I have to say, that was a pretty slick move with the reentry shield."

"Can't take credit," she replied. "Got the idea from the old Soviet cosmonaut program. There was an automatic landing system that kicked in if they tried to land in another country. As a precaution to keep them from overriding it, it also cut off their air. Remember all those 'tragic accidents' they had back in the sixties? That they stopped having once they started including an armed political officer in every crew."

"Where did you hear that?" Charley exclaimed.

"I didn't. My father couldn't figure out how so many could go wrong the same way, so he bought a bunch of old Soyuz capsules from museums and took them apart. They'd forgotten to take it out of one."

There was a silence.

"I think I'm sick," said Jack.

"Could be," said Stephen.

Jack stared at him. This was a very different man. Hearing a joke that was actually funny from him was just *weird*, like being mauled by a pack of hamsters.

"We'll be right over," Charley said, and started the thrusters. Now they worked.

"*Firebird*'s rolling," Marty said. "Damn, the shot went clean through! —The nanomachines must run on sunlight." He used his magnifier. "Yeah, the hole has black edges. I wonder why JNAIT isn't selling electric power?

They're not like silicon cells, they wouldn't have a problem with the doping getting sloppy before they generate enough power to build another."

"We're trying not to ruin anybody that doesn't insist on it," said a man's voice.

"How the— I'm not on an open channel."

"It may have come to your attention at some point that our pilot knows everything about how these vehicles work. You'd be Martin Tillery, right? I liked your paper on heat reclamation. I'm Mycroft Yellowhorse."

"The skydiver," Stephen said.

"And that'd be Stephen Edmundson, who broke an elbow qualifying for the U.S. team in '48. It's my guess that it was Samson Quinn who took the shot at us; fighter pilots have judgment issues. That leaves John Bernstein and Charles Loomis. Dr. Bernstein, if you'd joined the military your promotions would have been held up by the Pentagon and you'd never have made astronaut, which would be a damn shame since you're the smartest man in the corps. Commodore Loomis, the thing I find most interesting about you is that you were an extremely large baby."

"Ten pounds four ounces. You have that on *file*?"

"Not as such. Your middle name is Stuart, and you're the youngest in your family. Charles Stuart was the only king to be beheaded by the English. It's my guess you were overdue and a difficult birth."

"Three weeks. Nine hours followed by a Caesarean. I can see why they named you Mycroft."

"I chose that name. The name on my birth certificate was Guillaume Olivier Connors. Ten pounds seven, six weeks, more than thirty hours, no Caesarean. Sounds like your mother was nicer than mine. Of course, so was Medea. But I'm sorry I didn't have the bots ready for yours in time. You've suffered all your life from an illness inherited only through the maternal lineage. It's what I set out to cure when I started fooling with Toby's work. Say hi, Toby."

"Hi, Toby," said another man's voice.

"Gracie Allen lives," said Yellowhorse.

"Ohh *kay*then," Charley said, "braking now."

When they'd come to relative rest, Yellowhorse said, "Hang on a bit. I have to round up the help."

"Sure," said Charley.

Jack noticed Charley was slowly opening and closing his hands, looking at them.

"I didn't know you tried out for the Olympics," said Marty.

"Didn't just try out. Qualified. Only thing I ever had that wasn't handed to me, and it was taken away because I tripped over my own feet after I was down."

"This personality change of yours is making me want to check your pack for pods," Jack said.

Stephen looked at him. "I think I'm getting a rash where you sprayed me. It's all your fault. Does that help?"

"In a terribly wrong way, yes."

XXXV

They come to see; they come that they themselves may be seen.

—OVID

1

The entities aboard the interceptor watched with interested suspicion as *Envoy* disarmed itself and maneuvered close to *Firebird*. Sortie parties gathered the discarded materiel, which was examined with great care. Energetic and otherwise useful chemicals were separated and packaged, and the metals were stored for later processing.

Firebird stopped rolling. The two ships now had their bellies toward one another. Humans slowly got out of both ships, sending radio signals back and forth, and one from *Firebird* moved to attach a flexible connector between the ships' bellies. The connector presently altered shape in a way that indicated internal pressure.

The relative motion of the ships showed that *Envoy* was losing mass while *Firebird* gained it.

The interceptor had been designed to reach the ships, destroy *Envoy* if it attacked, repair *Firebird* if it was damaged, and get *Firebird* to Foundry safely. *Envoy* had attacked, but the sole attacker had immediately died, and none of the other humans had attempted further aggression. *Firebird* had been damaged, but manifestly had its own operators aboard, and was now intact. *Envoy*'s behavior indicated that the crew had surrendered to *Firebird*'s crew. *Firebird* was now refilled with oxidizer, though it would not have proportionate solid fuel to go with that.

The entities of the interceptor had been occupied with observation and preparedness for war. The value of having assigned some of them to construction of a communication system was now apparent. Lasers intended for making holes through *Envoy* were unsuited to the purpose, and in any case each could produce only one overwhelming shot before being remade, since it would destroy its own core as it fired.

A plan was formed as the humans from *Envoy* were making their way into *Firebird*. A chunk of metal from the discarded armaments was flung ahead of *Firebird*'s nose, then destroyed by a laser pulse, emitting light visible to humans. While the entities waited for the humans to respond—human movements were so slow as to be tiresome to watch—all entities not currently engaged in operations formed up in a layer on the side of the interceptor facing the ships.

2

May said, "Looking good, we've got another orbit before we need to *what* in *Hell* was *that*?" A searingly bright violet flare had appeared before the windshield, expanded at terrific speed as it cooled, still fluorescing, through the spectrum to red, and then vanished.

"Iron," said Mycroft, from outside. "Heated enough to strip all the electrons away, then take them back. About fifty milligrams, maybe. I noticed the colors seemed very pure, and I'd bet teeth there were exactly twenty-eight frequencies emitted as the electron shells filled back up. Four natural isotopes, seven shell states. I think the bots want our attention. —Yep. Look."

May switched a screen to the camera facing the bot ship. Bright yellow letters said WAIT.

"'Wait,'" said Mycroft. "Shall I wave to let them know we've seen it?"

"Go ahead."

The word promptly changed to YOU WILL; then, a moment later, BE MET. Then nothing.

WAIT YOU WILL BE MET.

May switched over to radar, which, aside from the automated alarm, was normally about as necessary and useful as a sniper scope on an automatic weapon. Something BIG was closing from higher orbit, with a thin stream of very fast stuff moving ahead of it.

The Rock was matching course.

"May, the bot ship is altering position to aft of *Envoy*. Now they're connecting that pipe to the tail and putting a shaft of something in. Ouch. *Way* in. Either they're going to salvage the solid fuel for us or they're checking its prostate."

"Any sign that they refrigerated the shaft first?"

"No, why would they do that?"

"Might have been a Pap test."

Mycroft made a strange noise in the back of his throat, but said nothing.

Finally got him.

Pretty much the first thing that Jack noticed was that two of the JNAIT astronauts appeared to be naked women.

The other NASA guys had noticed too. At least, they were all as quiet as Jack while they found seats and plugged their packs into the ship system.

After a while, Marty said to him, "I grew up in the wrong culture."

"Yah."

The man who must be Toby Glyer spoke: "I think JNAIT is probably going to be interested in hiring more astronauts. You might want to talk to Mycroft when he gets back in. —Sorry; Toby Glyer, Alice Johnson, May Wyndham piloting."

Charley pointed around and gave their names, then said, "So what's the word?"

"Currently it's 'nanos.' Although Mycroft calls them 'bots.' I think he begrudges the energy to use an extra syllable. He used to be just this side of an invalid."

"How come they turned him black and you red?" said Marty.

"He has his doing extra stuff, so they absorb more light. Red is what you get when he's authorized reconstruction."

"Reconstruction of what?"

"Whatever's been wearing out, starting with DNA. They also make vitamins, scavenge minerals, destroy bacteria, break down dead cells, and get rid of any tattoos you may have. And grow back missing body parts—most of them, anyway."

"You can modify what you look like, too," said Alice.

Jack suddenly placed her. "Hey, I remember reading about you."

"Don't point that finger at me, it might go off."

Jack held up his hand and wiggled his thumb, which had been parallel to his index finger. "No, see, the safety's on."

She grinned at that. "Okay."

"You got that from your grandfather," said Mycroft Yellowhorse over the radio.

Part of Jack's brain was interested to discover that gravity is not necessary for your jaw to drop. "How did you know that? How did you even know what I was doing?"

Mycroft laughed. "Your grandfather got it from me. He was my best friend in sixth grade. Funny, funny guy. We had mind-roasting contests before the term was coined. One time we were on a field trip to the local college to 'appreciate French culture,' and at lunch he coined the term 'Cheval Bourguignon.' We built model rockets together. Never got the damn things back. Jeff used to spray them with Scotchgard to cut friction. He could get more altitude out of an Alpha than Vernon Estes would have *believed*. Tell him 'Goc' said hello."

"I'm afraid he's dead. He wandered out of his nursing home last year, nobody ever found him."

"If it was in November, I suggest you look in Haiti. It's just barely possible for someone of sterling character to trigger the bot upgrade spontaneously through malnutrition, and from what I know of nursing homes and remember about Jeff, he might have done it, realized what was happening, and hit the road before he got put under a microscope. Haiti's turning out nice these days."

"You gave them to him too?"

"I gave them to everybody. Remember Goat Flu? Well—"

Jack spent the next little while listening to an astounding story.

Nobody interrupted.

XXXVI

Almost all people descend to meet.

—RALPH WALDO EMERSON

1

Foundry threw away more silicon to make final course alterations. The report from the interceptor made it clear that *Firebird* was repaired and refueled, and that *Envoy* qualified as salvage. Entities had been going through *Envoy* and found the design to be better than anything in the decoded records, so it would probably be worthwhile to make copies for human use.

The dead man had been found to be too thoroughly charred for the orientation of his brain connections to be reconstructed. That would have been useful.

Rendezvous was at hand. It was time to open contact.

2

"—If you pass this on, I will never tell you *anything interesting again*," Mycroft said. "Clear?" Everyone agreed, and he went on, "The bots guarantee that a woman who's aroused and capable of climax will have at least as good a time as her partner. The reason the Amish have an undiminished birthrate is that, as of November of '51, every woman who gets pregnant is one who actually wants a *child to raise*. Not 'proof of womanhood'; not a serf; not a household pet; not a live dress-up doll; not a talisman to save a bad marriage; not a puppet to impose ambitions on because your own were thwarted by someone doing the same thing to you when you grew up; not a punching bag. The Amish record on that score is unexcelled. — Which is not to say perfect, but you may rest assured that *everyone*'s record will be perfect in future. That is, everyone whose culture isn't extinct. Speaking of which, you don't have to worry about repercussions when you get back to America. I once met Tommie van Fossen, and I think he'll be decent about it."

"It's not the vice president we have to worry about," Charley said.

"He'll be president soon enough. I'm amazed he's not already. Haven't you heard what I've been saying about the bots? Robert Foster cannot possibly manifest the attitude that made him so acceptable to his Party—and he surely does—without mainlining some heavy painkillers and anticonvulsives, and he is not a man who comprehends proportion or self-control. He'll certainly OD or be a vegetable before the election. —As I was saying, van Fossen is an honest man, possibly included as an attempt to balance the ticket. You're good."

After a pause for shocked absorption of this, Charley said, "Do you mind if we at least send a message to warn him? An officer takes an oath."

"I quite understand, and have not the slightest objection. Bear in mind that you want to send a message, to a powerful man, whose way of coping with the phenomenon of immediate and protracted agony, whenever he does something he knows to be wrong, and *only* on those occasions, is to take increasingly large doses of narcotics; the aforesaid message being that all he has to do to stop the pain is to cease to do evil, such as, say, having people murdered when he hears something that upsets him, a category which extends down to the word 'no.' Let me know when you've worked out the phrasing that you think will do him some good. I'll contact my own people and have your families and friends and pets and keepsakes and so forth moved somewhere safe before you send it, shall I?" Mycroft stood attentively—well, floated attentively—before Charley, with his hands laced before his stomach, wide-eyed, smiling, his head at a slight angle, the very embodiment of guileless solicitude.

The really appalling thing was that Charley was certain that if he, Charley Loomis, was silly enough to insist on sending that message, Mycroft Yellowhorse would do exactly as he had offered. "Do you always work stuff out that fast?" he said.

"He does," said Toby. "He used to do it sometimes even when he was sick. I thought for a while that he was using the nano network to augment his thinking, but from what he's described it'd only be good for calculations."

"*Only?*" said Jack. "If I'm following this, this guy put an experimental machine into his own cells, then got himself sentenced to death because he knew he'd survive being killed horribly, so he'd be put away for life without parole, just so he'd have time and a place to design a better machine to experiment on himself with? Which he could do without funding, lab facilities, or a pencil for making notes, because of the nanomachine network in him, and you're brushing it off as 'only' calculations?"

"Also simulations and memory search," Mycroft pointed out, clearly willing to take up the mind-roasting tradition with a new generation of the family.

"What about coordination?" said Stephen. He sounded suspicious.

"Not so much. They have to work by monitoring the feedback in the system they're working with, and that operates at the same speed it always did. Are you thinking of the parachute landing? The net let me know what

I had to do, but I had to do it. The fact that the bots cured everything that kept me from getting into perfect physical condition does enter into it."

After a moment, Stephen said, "Oh. —Sorry."

"It's okay. —It sounds like you might be starting late in life to find a balance between accusation and accountability. It does take a while; believe me, I know. —On the bright side, you have more time to perfect it than you used to. I think you'll do okay. I've been watching your character improve just since you got here. You might find it helpful to read the works of Robert Heinlein and Poul Anderson. The hallmark of a truly great philosopher is that he never writes books on philosophy, and those two—"

"We're there," said May.

"Yay. —Are the best. Anderson for how to get along with people who are conspicuously wrong, and Heinlein for when not to. —Okay, let's see if they'll talk now."

"They think," Toby heard Edmundson say. "Do they have souls?"

"I don't see why not," Mycroft said. "Cats certainly do; watch one for a day. Souls seem to be contagious."

"Everybody shut up, will you?" Toby said. His nerves were ragged. The nanos had clustered together for better processing, as he had designed them to, and he had contemplated the possibility that they would become conscious; but he hadn't considered for an instant that they would toss out their basic programming and do things as wildly different as they already had.

He had no idea of their intentions. Neither did Mycroft, but it didn't seem to worry *him*.

The communication board lit up: laser light coming in.

The voice that the message was in was warm, human, and likable. And familiar. It sounded remarkably like Walt Disney. "Greetings, *Firebird*. This is Foundry. We would like to speak with Toby Glyer."

After a false start where nothing came out, Toby said, "Speaking."

"Dr. Glyer, it is good to hear you directly. You gave us life and purpose, and provided us with materials, fuel, and knowledge. Foundry consists principally of metals and carbon, sorted, separated, and ready for industrial processes of your choosing. We consider this a fair trade. We now wish to discuss the rate of payment for future deliveries."

Toby was saved from having to think of an immediate reply by Mycroft's loud laughter.

He got it partly under control, then said, "I'll go deliver payment for the next couple of installments. You explain. —Major, they are initiating an act of commerce. I'll go out on a limb and say 'yes' —they have souls."

As Mycroft went through the air lock, Toby began telling the nanos of Foundry about the value of exchanging design features. It helped that *Firebird* had two couples aboard; he could give examples.

XXXVII

Love is that condition where someone else's happiness is necessary to your own.

—ROBERT ANSON HEINLEIN

One of the humans came out of the cargo bay and threw something at the base of Foundry's radio antenna. It stuck and spread. It consisted of more operators, which had clustered themselves into entities.

Entities they didn't know.

The entities of Foundry and the new entities established a mode of communication, and began exchanging information at once. The new entities were different in structure, and had useful features that the Briareus crew hadn't come up with. Most began making arrangements for the design of new and improved entities at once.

One telescope-based cluster remained in place, watching the human who had made the delivery until he went back inside.

She thought he seemed happy.

Prudence is the belief that bad things have preventable causes.

Paranoia is the belief that it's all the same cause.

Politics is the belief that you know what the cause is.

Sometimes you do.

—WILLIAM CONNORS

TOR

Voted
#1 Science Fiction Publisher
25 Years in a Row

by the *Locus* Readers' Poll

———————•———————

Please join us at the website below
for more information about this
author and other science fiction,
fantasy, and horror selections, and to
sign up for our monthly newsletter!

www.tor-forge.com